A DAUNTING JAUNT

GERIE REVEUR

DEDICATION

This book is dedicated to all those who labored hard to see the fruition of my work. It was a long ride coming up with this artistry, but I thank everyone for not simply watching by. So, to my parents, siblings, and all the characters in this book, who didn't feel offended. I know I replaced your wonderful names with French versions, but, well …

CONTENTS

Acknowledgments   i

Prologue   ii

ACKNOWLEDGMENTS

I cannot say for sure that this work would have come to see the light of day, were it not for everyone who stood by me. I have been in part, assisted by several people, both in-house and from the outside. Writing a list of their names would be hectic. But, all in all, I would like to say thank you.

I am also grateful in advance to all those who will find pleasure in reading my book. The main motivation behind my writing was for the world to hear out my story, and come to understand my situation. In addition, all the characters in my work are very real, so, it was an honor telling their story through my eyes.

In as much as there have been people around to support me, I would like to thank Amazon, for creating a great platform for self-publishing. It is though their generous support, that the world is reading my story for the first time. *Merci beacoup*!

PROLOGUE

I feel excited about the invite
I humbly take the offer as if it is right
At the step of the way, I get carried away
But, the clever lady draws away from me, beforehand
I am left with the urge to go on

The trip goes on as planned
And I get to sample the marvels
Hey, the mother in nature is truly remarkable
I get to live in a temporary fantasy
The facade is just too luring

Across the Kenyane heartland,
The jaunt seems all to daunting
Not very enchanting but,
All too exciting.

That exciting jaunt seems to lose its appeal
Realizing everything is not black and white,
I get to see the bigger picture,
The world from what it truly is
I learn to not escape my reality.
I learn to accept myself.
All in my daunting jaunt.
Gerie Reveur

The sky was full and robust. The birds were singing their merry songs. I walked with a lot of zeal. The road to the corridor I was walking into was very dusty. It had not rained in forever. Ever since January, it was as dry as the mouths of the starving kids in Turkana. They did go hungry for months. No one cared about their well being. The churchmen said they were cursed. Others said they were stupid for not being vigilant and running away from their poverty. I reckoned they should've just skipped town and gone to Naïrobi. It was the land of opportunities, so why not? I thought. I did thank the *Nations Unies* for their humanitarian efforts over there.

I had not been in contact with any woman for the past four months. I stared at women passing by me with lust. Cacaoyer had a diverse bunch. From all shades, I could see them. Most of them were Quicouyu. Apart from the usual stereotypes condemning them of being cons, the one I liked the most was that of them having one of the most beautiful women in the country. I did like them. I could swear that after reading the book, Decolonizing the mind by Ngugi wa Thiong'o, I would have changed my perspective on colonialism. Well, I didn't do it per se. The society had set standards that the lighter the skin, the better the woman. I couldn't argue with tradition, so I followed along.

A few hours earlier my cousin had promised me a road trip to my father's birthplace. I had been there when I was sixteen. Ten years later, I knew everything had changed. Considering it was upcountry, most of my peers would be grown, parents. 'Ha-ha', I laughed at the sound of that. The corridor started getting narrower. It seemed that with every step I was almost close. I had agreed with him to pick up my stuff and meet up at his place after three hours. I figured that would give me time to say my goodbyes to my brother, Ami.

After finishing school, he had opted to live on his own. The sweet part of it all was that his lady co-worker was his roommate. He was against the idea of living with her at first. However, I cunningly convinced him to accept the offer. After all, he would be bringing his girlfriend over and there was no real harm since he worked in the nights. I planned to seize that vacuum and date that girl for good. We had even agreed to live together. That would be one of my easiest sexual adventures. I would not even sweat for it. I would have a girl with me just like that.

I reached for the gate door handle, which was not opening. Darn it! There was a lock. The insecurity in the area had prompted the landlord to come up with extra security measures. Everyone had to carry their key. I called his phone and after a few minutes, he came. He wore a white vest which showed his bulging muscles. We had started working out on strength training five years before, but it seemed that he was the one taking it too far. With the title of 'Body Builder of The Year', he had to maintain his reputation by adding the extra bulk with food supplements—*I hated them for I feared they might contain steroids.*

"Oh, you are here brother. Tell me you're not going to chicken out from this deal. I hate chickens?"

"Ha-ha brother. Tell me you're kidding. I do hate goats and their kids."

We all laughed at our wordplay as we entered the small settlement. It was owned by a pastor and managed by his wife. And so, as you might have guessed, there were very strict rules. For one, they had to know the number of guys who were living in the house. There was a line of bathrooms next to the gate and five rows of houses with about ten units for each. His unit was on the second house to the left. As a guy who loved the style, I hated their architecture. They cost only 3,500 Kenya Shillings per month. That was way too low for a decent house. It had a wooden door, and the walls were made of corrugated iron sheets. I didn't like it, but my sexual desires had driven me to do so by default. It's not like I had any other choice.

Once inside, there was a disassembled bed and two mattresses. One was lying on the floor, with a girl on top of it, while the other had been tied and hung from the roof. Before I, was a girl I had been dying to meet for a while. She had long hair and a beautiful face. Her eyes were whitish and largely round. They drove fire in me. I looked at her without mention. My brother was busy getting ready for work. He had gone to the gym early in the morning and then had taken a nap, until when I had unceremoniously woken him up. He polished clean his shoes, shaved his beard, and then wore his black suit. He then bid us farewell.

I had taken the time to introduce myself to the girl and know her before Ami had left. She said her name was Jeanne. I complimented her for having a wonderful name, but deep down I knew it sucked. I looked at her eyes longingly and then started getting to know her better after he had left. She seemed nice, but I knew I had the upper hand there. I cursed myself for not having carried protection that day. In my presence was a girl lying comfortably next to me without any sight clue who I was. Throngs of fire were hitting me from my every nerve. My early social education classes had taught me to abstain and run away from every moment that would pose a temptation to me. I had to think fast. If I didn't act clever I would end up impregnating an innocent girl, or contract an incurable STI.

She said she worked as a steward at a nightclub with my brother.

At least that was where they met. I felt a sudden urge to be the listener as she told me her story. She recounted how she had lived in the ghetto as a child and then studied in non-formal schools. Her family had condemned her profession and termed her a prostitute. I even suspected she might have been HIV positive. As a rookie shrink, I prided myself in mind-control. I could study a person's micro-expressions and general behavior, that would allow me to say things that would manipulate their actions. I did that a lot, and I was sorry for her for what I would do next.

As she talked, I noticed her being fidgety and playful with a bunch of keys. One of the oldest tricks in the book for getting your way with a woman was through bodily contact. If I touched her, I would create some communication. I held on to her hand and then noticed my body getting warm. I drew my hand back and then thought of something else. In her talk, she had mentioned that if I moved in, I would sleep with my brother on the bed, and she would take the floor. I talked of being gentlemanly, but she insisted that the cool breeze seeping in from under the door was better for her.

I wittingly crept onto the mattress and told her I wanted to try out her luxury. She looked at me with a look that said get-outta-here, but at the same time, she was very welcoming of me. I wondered how a girl in her early twenties would suddenly agree to move in with a random guy she had just met. On top of where I lay, I had mixed feelings of guilt and hard-heartedness. I had promised my girlfriend from my rural home, before I had left for the city, that I would remain faithful. She had placed all her trust in me. And there I was, about to play her. I placed my hand on Jeanne's waist and then let it rest there for a while. She was wearing a black trench-coat and stockings. I guessed she did that intentionally for she was alone.

Her talk now moved from normal to timider. I was used to the latter whenever I brought in girls into my house. Dark thoughts started flowing into my mind. Since I had no protection, I would simply caress her and have several French kisses, that would be it. It had been about fifteen minutes since I had gotten there, but all seemed like an eternity. However, my perfect bliss ended when she drew my hand away from her waist and then said she wasn't ready for any intimacy then. I felt bad that my ego had been crushed, but I couldn't do anything. The lady had decided. I had to be a gentleman. I slowly looked at my phone and then said I had seven minutes left before I had to pack.

I felt equally proud that she had some sort of dignity inside her. It didn't take long before I finally convinced her to escort me to the next street from her place. In her, I saw a mature woman who was fed up with the tricks from men. She was somehow looking for a serious relationship, which I was not ready to offer her.

I parted ways with her along a dusty road. She wore on her, pink sandals. Her trench-coat viciously displayed her bodily curves. Her dimples made her even more beautiful. I could swear that as I was walking with her, I wasn't concentrating on anything else but her posteriors. She walked with that swagger which was common with women from Luo Lac. I had no other alternative but to follow along. I had hoped that she would look at me and catch a final glimpse but to no avail. I wondered how I had gotten a renewed interest in women the more I got older. I had managed to control my sexual desires while in college. My tools of trade were study and exercise. However, it seemed that their appeal was fading the more I was away from the academic circles. I knew I had to do something, but I had not figured that out. It pained me that my bodily desires were taking their toll.

I had lost count of whatever was happening around me. There were people of all sorts, trying to make a living. From women trying to grab my attention with second-hand clothes, to men trying hard to sell roasted groundnuts. There was no hassle that would pull me. I simply walked by. It was around five in the evening. I lived by the clock and strongly believed that delaying time was not in my genes. I had planned to pick up my clothes for thirty minutes at most. I knew my mother would be home any moment from then. It would have been great if she were not there, I thought. That would have made me invisible. I would then explain my sudden journey to her later. I didn't want her to make any fuss about it.

Just as I arrived home, to that single room house, she got in. it was like fate had planned everything out. I sat on a chair next to the door. I had chosen it specifically for study. The place was modest. With a couch on the left, a bed on the right, and a wall cabinet on the opposite end, it was a full house. Her two sons and I, plus her, struggled to fit into that tiny space. We were grateful that she only came over during the weekends. She slept on the bed with the younger son, while the older one took the couch. As a man who cared less, I curled myself up on the chair. I found it uncomfortable most of the time, so I had to crash at my friends' houses whenever I got the chance. The road trip had come as a blessing in disguise.

She struggled to pull in a five-pound sack of maize to the house. With the massive seats blocking her path, I had to help her out. Her average-sized tiny frame denied her the strength to do menial tasks. I came to the rescue. I started pulling my clothes from a rope tied across the room. A curtain that hung from it acted as a makeshift wall, which separated the house into a living and bedroom. The far corner was used as the kitchen. It was small but fully utilized. I packed up everything, in my backpack, and then tried to remember the essentials I might have forgotten. I stalled for a few minutes and then told her I would be leaving for a week. From what I had learned in the past not doing so would render me homeless.

I had just graduated two years before. Having worked as a volunteer, my monthly stipends were not that much. I had to survive off from her. She didn't mind but I had to keep up with her nagging and constant self-righteousness. I had once left and lived on my own for a year and a half. Once life had gotten the better of me, I had to go upcountry and live there for five months. Realizing that my bachelor's degree was going to waste, I came back to her like the prodigal son. She was very accepting of me. However, it was very like her to tell me never to act stupid again. I had to follow her lead, but deep down I cursed myself for being twenty-five and super broke. I had sent countless applications to firms, but none of them ever replied to me. I had lost all hope, and after quitting my volunteer job, well… I had to hustle hard. I earned not more than five dollars a week. Since she had agreed to pay for the rent; it was my responsibility to buy food and prepare it for her sons.

"Okay, you can leave,"

That was it, not even a complete sentence. I expected her to at least ask me where, but I had already given up on my conscious self-questioning. Ever since she had parted ways with my father, when I was three, she cared less about him. I lived with him until I was seventeen. That was when I asked daddy who my real mommy was. He was quick to take me where she was. Her first order of business was to preach to me about there being one God, Jesus. Her arguments were very convincing, not that I was doubtful. I followed along because whenever we met up, she gave me two hundred shillings. That was a lot. I would get myself snacks and buy my friends gifts. It pained me how she showed up later in my life. In spite of all that, my monetary greed took the best of me.

The dark was slowly kicking in, which made movement a nightmare in the poorly lit road. I knew if I delayed much longer, I would get robbed. I carried with me my smartphone, headphones, and laptop. As an aspiring software developer and freelance writer, those were invaluable tools. If they were to be stolen, I would be done for. I saw faint lights from the shops I passed by. With the roads under construction; I had to knock with my feet the occasional stray rocks in my path. I liked to converse deeply with myself and have internal reflections. They helped me get by my troubled life. I knew I had talent but my fear was it going to waste. After crossing several streets I was finally at my cousin's house.

His very lifestyle was proof of his success. He had finished college when I was through with my O'Levels. He was now a celebrated attorney. With too much cash at his disposal, the only thing he could do was entertain his relatives with liquor and feed them to their fill. I bit my lip hard whenever I went to his place. I knew he was throwing to my face his wealth and not offering to do anything helpful to my situation. He had promised me a job two years before but it seemed like it was all wishful thinking. I kept urging him on and on to consider it. However, I finally gave up after a while of futile effort. I had to do what other people did when they got to his place, eat and drink. For my case, though, I drank coffee and tea. I strictly avoided alcohol.

I found him in his house alone. He had two bottles of whiskey on his table. He lived in a single bedroom house with a living room, bathroom, and kitchen. I liked his interior décor style. He had a contemporary set of couches, a home theater, and a ridiculously large flat-screen TV, which was mounted on the wall. Next to it was a water dispensing machine. The bedroom had a king-size bed. Whoever sang the song California King Bed had his in mind. He was just getting started with his drink when I arrived. I looked around and took my stuff to his bedroom. He was chanting to the loud blaring music he was playing. It consisted of contemporary pop culture and traditional African ethnic fusion. He unsuccessfully invited me to join him in his drinking spree, to which I politely declined.

I went to the kitchen and prepared myself a cup of coffee. Since he had been sensible enough to buy training weights, I started working out my shoulders, biceps, and triceps. It was a form of therapy which helped me escape from my misery. For once, I saw myself in control. I forgot all about my poverty and concentrated on building my physical health. It took me three hours before I realized I had been exhausted. I stood upright and then looked at myself. I was only in my boxer shorts. That made me practically naked. I washed up quickly and then started checking my emails, and social media. My cousin, Jacques, had succumbed to sleep. With no one else at least conscious around, I reached for the kitchen cupboard and took two cups of rice, and several handfuls of macaroni. I cooked the food for about fifteen minutes before I hungrily gobbled it. It looked plentiful, but I managed to finish it.

My life living in poor settlements had taught me to never waste a chance at a good life. I saw a hot shower option in the bathroom. After what seemed like an eternity, I felt like staying in that small paradise forever. My body was, however, getting damp, with all the water passing over me, I decided to end it. What followed was a session of watching satellite TV channels for the better part of the night. My recklessness prompted me to take off my pants. Just as I was about to enter a state of madness, there was a knock at the door. Upon closer inspection, it was a boy who sold natural gas cylinders at the gate. He came all packed. I initially thought it would be a two-man trip, I had been wrong.

"Hey, Étienne I need a cup of porridge, please do prepare it," Jacques said.

He stood up from his slumber in white sweat pants and a vest. His drunkenness had prompted him to hydrate. I felt pity for the guy who came in only to be given work. He didn't seem to mind. He quickly jumped to his task without any complaints. His talking style was like that of a girl. I was tempted to laugh at him. However, my concentration on his actions faded as soon as sleep started taking over my will. I lay fast asleep on the couch, not minding about my surroundings. Before I knew it, I was in dreamland.

I always hated my sleep cycles, they were bound to make me scared always. At one time back, I dreamt that I was stranded in a winding road in a valley, I didn't know how I got there. Behind me was a group of assailants, who all carried machetes and golf clubs in either hand. That was enough for me to make a run for my life. As I ran, I could not hear their voices, it was like watching a scene of Marilyn Monroe's film, Some Like It Hot.

Everything was all black and white. It's like the concept of color never had any meaning in human dreams. Before I knew it, morning had come. That particular dream always recurred in my sleep whenever I was depressed. However, that time was different. I had no reason to be scared. In fact, I was happy.

I saw myself inside a virtual reality machine. I got to have conversations with the avatars of real-life virtual assistants like Cortana, Alexa, Siri, and the Google Assistant. I ruled the digital divide as an overlord for a brief moment, before everything went black. I saw myself in oblivion. I had gotten scared to the point that scary didn't have any special meaning to me. That got me thinking, maybe the end of me would be like that. Like a downward spiral, my fantasy began to fade away in flashes.

I saw myself falling into an infinite pit. The fall continued getting deeper. Bobby Ray's song, 'Don't Let Me Fall,' kept ringing in my head. I looked left and then right; sadly there was no one to come to my aid. Before I knew it, I heard Jacques tell Étienne that I should wake up. I rolled around the mattress I slept on. The floor was less chilly as compared to the one I crashed in at my Mama's house. Having showered the previous night, I jumped into brushing my teeth. They told me to hurry, but my slowness got the better of me. I was tasked with arranging floor tiles at the back of the car and then opening the gate.

I had very high expectations for the journey. However, in as much as I was enthusiastic of a dream jaunt, I knew the people on the other end would not welcome me with open arms. My father had left his ancestral home back when he was a teen. He had forgone his right to own a part of his father's land. Instead, he had chosen to buy one in the *Vallée de Rift* highlands. That had doomed him and me to being forever visitors over there. The other thing was that my cousin had success written all over him. Having completed college, he had graduated with a degree in law. He had been a smart guy. During his heydays, he used to ace all his tests. On the contrary, being four years his junior (*at least academically, age-wise—not very much*), I was the train-wreck.

I had graduated from college, but the way I earned my living was questioned by many—*I could swear my ways were always legit*. I worked at a children's home as a teacher. My boss was one of the best. I secretly wished I could call him my parent. I survived on the school-food they offered me. That gave me some bit of leverage at home. God knows what would happen if my mother were to provide everything for me. People would not stop talking. In spite of all that they all did. Most of them wondered why I would stoop so low and work for a wage that would equal that of someone who had never gone to school, let alone college.

My worst fear was meeting up the guys there at home. By the time Jacques had extended his invitation, I was full of excitement. However, it all faded once I thought of its possible outcomes. They would quickly laugh their hearts out when they saw me in my state. Word had already gone round that I had borrowed my cousin's clothes from top to bottom, even the undies. I had walked the Naïrobien streets with brown envelopes every morning, delivering my resume to prospective organizations, with the hope of a way out. All that was unfortunately futile. My pants had been worn out, I couldn't sit with my legs apart—*that would have been an epic humiliation*. My socks had been torn all over, and my shoes had their soles completely erased out. It was like walking on slippers.

My father had been one of the richest sons in his homestead, back in the day—*some have said continually that with success comes failure*. He had been swallowed into the pleasures of the world. Alcohol and women were the best of his friends, and in no time, he had fathered more than a dozen kids with different wives. All was at stake, for his old age couldn't let him make money like before. Lots of responsibilities came in and he failed to keep up. Before he knew it, he was a deadbeat. The village laughed at him in silence, even those that were miserable found solace in his suffering. They praised themselves for being poor all along than having prosperity fade away while they saw it.

Most people had considered me as the family savior. All the other children had very little hopes in life. The older ones had become full-fledged drug addicts and sex machines, with their only survival in casual work. The girls had faced the fate of early pregnancies, and had no other option but to throw their infants at their father's doorstep. The younger ones alike were following the family trend. When I saw how alcoholism had messed up our family, I bit my lip and swore to never consume it in my life. I had made many enemies over time because of that simple decision.

I knew that the villagers would get their taste of criticism once I got there. Their highlight would be, 'Savior Son Gone Broke or ...' they would have better neologisms for that. I had heard rumors that most of them criticized my earlier choice of taking up Philosophy and Literature as a degree. They were so into traditional professions that they failed to see the bigger picture. I hoped I would get a job soon.

We used the new Jointures Road route that took to Quicouyu. The plan was to take a detour from the bypass around town, and then head for Naïvasha and not the CBD. Jacques's choice was to use the Eau Chaude road. I felt a little elated when we cruised along the Karen suburb. I asked myself silently if I had done anything wrong to the gods and all divinity. I was born into poverty despite my father having cash. My mother had left him due to some random idea she had of him being unfaithful—*to a larger extent, I would agree to disagree.* What would follow was me and her other sons repeatedly starving for most of the time. By the time I was old enough to talk, I would take to the streets and beg for my nourishment. I was so close to the street kids around that they showed me a cool spot, it was the Sang Précieux Girls' Secondary School. They served needy kids boiled maize and beans. I survived on that until I was four.

I saw a family go to their SUV car. A happy quartet of well-dressed children and their parents. In the background was a house worker packing lunches in the kids' back-packs. I felt a little jealous, knowing that during my time, the concept of lunch was a dream. I held onto my fingers as tears slowly rolled down my cheeks. Jacques and Étienne didn't notice my turmoil. They had taken the front seats and were busy in their chit and chatter.

The vehicle we were traveling in was an ordinary salon car. I disliked our driver's taste in automobiles. I would have recommended him to buy a manlier car, like an SUV or a high end Mercedes Benz. The road was getting smoother and smoother as we headed deep into the highway. The car started to accelerate in speed. Before we knew it, we had already hit fifty, eighty, and finally a hundred miles per hour. We relaxed ourselves to old school hip hop and RnB music of the 90s and early 2000s. I slowly hummed to Kanye West's lyrical rhymes. The journey seemed to get the better of me at first. I hadn't taken any breakfast due to my one rule of never eating while journeying.

Jacques had said that the real road trip would start once we had left Naïrobi. True to his words it did. Once we reached Naïvasha county, the beauty began. Since it was the dry season, the whole landscape was yellow and welcoming. On our road to Naïvasha, what scared me the most was riding along the escarpments. They were frightening and electrifying at the same time. I held my breath as vans sped past us at full speed. I wondered what kind of sane person would endanger their lives. It was no wonder our country had experienced a world-record of tragic road carnage in the past.

I had heard earlier of our government's ongoing Standard Gauge Railway (SGR) project. It started to make sense to me when I saw the huge metallic snake winding its way across the dry grassland. I assumed it must have been expensive. Judging from the unforgiving *Vallée de Rift* terrain, it must have cost the government a fortune. It was dry to the point that I could literally choke on the dust seeping its way through the slightly opened car window, on my side.

I was never much of small-talk kind of a person. As Jacques and Étienne conversed, I kept silent at the back. It's not like I preferred to be so, but the unfortunate rules of Darwin had subjected my genetic makeup to be so. I looked at my smartphone and later turned it off. I was not ready to let my consciousness be controlled by some 'white' man's device—*pun intended*. Most of my peers were glued 24/7 to their gadgets. It had been a revolution of how back in the day, people were TV zombies and now zombies of all kinds. Our lives were constantly under the influence of everything electronic around us. I wished we could turn back the time. Back to the good old days, when the entertainment was performing arts in the theaters. That would be the greatness needed.

"Oh, look! That guy driving that Subaru car is over speeding …"

"It won't be long before he is noticed by the Naroque police,"

Étienne had responded to Jacques's sudden emotive burst. The car driving past us was sleek and remarkable in all aspects. It had a shiny midnight black shade. From its rear, we could see the words, *Sex is not the Answer* …, inscribed on it. I laughed at Jacques's assumption of the subject not being the answer, but it being the question, and yes being the answer. I bowed my head in disappointment. If people would have been creative in solving the problems ravaging our country, just like they did in erotic puzzlers, then we would have become a developed nation.

Naïvasha had a boring landscape. The only appealing things in it were acacia trees, wild zebras, and shrubs, which were scattered everywhere. I looked forward to reaching Naroque. In front of us was a sign that said, 'Welcome to Naroque County'. On my far left was the famous Jointures Hills. When in Naïrobi, I could see them at a far distance (*they looked all blue and blurry*). Surprisingly, they all looked the same from where I was. The road we were in was a single lane. From that point we drove smoothly, I could guess that it had been recently constructed. The landscape started becoming less of acacia trees and more of bare plains. It was quite understandable that that was the home of the Masai people. If anyone from abroad were to talk about Africa, then those guys would be the topic of discussion. To be honest, I never fancied the way they lived. 'For crying out loud, we were in the 21st century. It made less sense for a people to live in the ways of way back,' I thought.

I had never gotten a shot at true love ever in my life. Back then, when I was a teen, I had heard of people getting into relationships, I tried but to no avail. My hugest stumbling block, ever since I went to high school, was my delayed physical growth and super skinny physique. So, whenever I approached girls, they would be full of excuses. One of the greatest highlights in my life was getting rejected by a naïve girl in high school. She supposedly thought I wasn't tall enough. I have grown to hate any girl with the name, Gertrude, ever since. After growing several inches taller, it was no longer my height, but my baby-face, as they used to call it. The latter harassed me until my young adult days—*even having a beard wasn't enough.*

Aside from my occasional ups and downs, I had something, which I didn't know how to call. I had met up with a pretty girl, whom I had had a crush on. We never got to second base, and the far we got was writing each other letters. We never got past that. That was the only kind of relationship my childish mind had ever known. I have never met that girl ever since. I was mostly drawn to simplicity in my life. With time I got a little afraid of approaching girls who seemed flashy.

My family had acquired land in Naküru back then when I was six. I often visited there whenever we had family road trips. It had become a habit going over there that the place seemed like a second home. Little did I know that there was something good in store for me. I was sixteen then and at that stage, my adolescent mind had taken its toll. I had perfected my speaking skills with girls by then. In as much as I was good at talking, that never got me past the pity hug. Yes, those girls were pitiful of me. It seemed like they were sorry for not having a relationship with me.

The place we were living in was full of hills. It was previously known as the White Highlands. It was always chilly over there. I had to wear heavy jackets most of the time. My father had dropped me off in his farmhouse and promised he would come to pick me up after the school holidays. I was left under the care of my aunt. She was fun, but not that amusing to me. The only thing I could do in that uncivilized place was sleep, train in martial arts, and take walks. Since the place was grassy, it was better walking in sandals than in closed shoes.

I left our gate in a hurry. I was eager to leave and explore the outside before dusk. The road was lined with a boulevard of Douglas fir trees. As I walked I admired the fenced farms, most of them were not more than five acres. People were busy in their work, and none of them took notice of me as I walked by. I felt a sudden urge to lay down on the ground and fall asleep. It was never one of my highlights to get bored to death in the middle of nowhere.

As I was beating myself up about boredom, a girl passed by me. Judging from her looks, she was about fourteen. I knew that was my moment to shine. She was just my type, her swag was off the charts. She had short, well combed, and oiled hair. Her skin tone was brownish and to my delight, I was slightly taller. Being around 5'6", I guessed she would be two inches shorter than me. I was quick to notice that she wore sandals like me, held a plastic bag in her hand, and also balanced a bucket full of cornflour on her head. I tried to catch a glimpse of her face, but she was too shy to let me to. I was left with no other option but to get close to her.

"Hello there, how are you doing?"

«Je vais bien merci.»

"Aha, so you speak French. I like that. *«Je ne comprends le francais pas, vous parlez lentement.»* "

I looked at her with a mixed feeling of happiness and fear at the same time. It would have been a huge drawback if things went south and the girl rejected me. I would never ever forgive myself. I tried very much for our encounter not to be a pain in the head for her. From what I could gather, she was getting uneasy. It was a good thing that she had not left yet. She had stood transfixed to the ground as if she was petrified. At that moment we stole glances at each other, while still convincing ourselves we were not doing so. I was always shy whenever I saw people at the eye level. However, none of us blushed. It seemed like we were communicating effectively through our body language than a conversation would accomplish.

"Hi, I'm sorry for bothering you at this time. My name is Reveur. It is an honor meeting you."

"Mine too. I am Félicité of the highlands. You look new around here. Tell me, where are you from?"

I felt my heart jump to my vocal cords in a good way. I could feel the proverbial butterflies fill my stomach. It was the first time witnessing a girl express interest in me. She was different from the other girls, for she didn't play hard to get. She looked cool and composed. She wore a thick cotton skirt with African prints on it. Her legs were slender and less hairy. She wore on her, a brightly colored blouse and a white headscarf. Whenever I would meet a beautiful girl, desires would take hold of me, but for her, it was something magical. I felt a sudden urge to know her better and be her protector. She seemed like the quiet kind, the type that I associated myself with.

"I am not from around here. I am from the big city. I recently came here a few days ago. I can't say that I did like it here, but now, I have changed my perspective."

She looked at me briefly and then smiled. She had those eyes that grabbed my attention. I liked that whenever I talked she would occasionally throw in a smile and then fidget her fingers. I had never had a good listener ever, so that was a good start. We had met in the afternoon but before we knew it, it had already gotten dark. I looked around, and there was no one in sight. She slowly held on to my hand and then signaled to me that it was time to go home. It took us about half an hour to reach her place. After receiving a light hug, we bid each other farewell.

«*Bonne soirée mademoiselle,*» I said.

The pitch dark evening denied me the chance to see her one more time. I followed her movements until she was no more than a silhouette. I had carried with me a small burner phone. It was a good thing it had a handy clock and internet connectivity. The place was dark and frightening, but I braced myself for any danger that would befall me. I was open to anything. The events that happened that day had left a strong impact on the universal timeline. I would be more than happy to live within that loop.

After what seemed like a moment of eternity, I found myself in the car. We were approaching a roadblock. The others had taken no notice of my daydreaming. At the side of the road was the over speeding Subaru car. Jacques smiled at himself proudly as he pointed at the car. He said the guy had sped past 94 mph, which was beyond the limit for the Kenyane Highway regulation. I knew he would have to crash around the area and await a court hearing a few days later. It was tough not following rules for Kenyanes.

"Hey man, why have you been daydreaming. Are you apt on not sucking in this beautiful scenery? What the..."

I looked at Jacques and then acted dumb. He increased the stereo volume and continued with his drive. I had lost count of how many times he had asked me something and I ignored. They had gotten used to my attitude and had put their full focus on the road. The drive across Naroque was getting more interesting. There were water pans all over. It was funny that with the prolonged dry spell, the pans were still packed with water. I could also notice the wheat plantations around the area were very large. The farmers had started tilling their land. Once the rains had begun, they would be all set for their planting season.

There was much I learned about the Masai peoples. Most of them had moved away from their traditional lifestyle. They had started sending their kids to school and even constructed modern houses. I liked the fact that modernism had caught up with them without them noticing it. Once we arrived in Naroque town, I saw it as small but slightly developed. At one place were a pizzeria, a patisserie, and a coffee shop. I bit my lip with regret. I wished I never had that rule of not eating while journeying. We didn't make a stop there anyway. The more we left Naroque, the greener the landscape became. I had to accustom myself to that new change.

The day we were traveling was Palm Sunday. I hadn't known much about the Catholic religion. As a liberal religionist, I only used their sign of the cross in my prayers before meals. A few miles later, we reached Propriété town. The Catholic faithful had carried palm fronds all over. It was like the place was swarming with a colony of churchmen. We had left our windows open to let in a cool breeze. Little did we know our choice had not been the best. The leaves started flowing in from all directions. Jacques pressed a button at the side of his door, all the doors automatically closed. We had to wait for an hour before the road cleared.

I wondered why Propriété county was greener than most of the country. It seemed like it was getting a greater share of rain than the other parts of the region. We didn't get to enjoy the place because of the overly sparse settlements and underdevelopment. I looked forward to reaching Ressentir county. According to Jacques, it was the land of God's tears. In his point of view, the place rained relentlessly even when the rest of the country was as dry as a poor man's lips.

As we approached the border to Ressentir, Jacques mentioned that the area was a hotspot for the infamous 2007/2008 Kenyane post-election violence—*the one which claimed the lives of scores of innocent souls*. He argued that a Kalenjin strongman had been killed in Ressentir territory. That alone was enough to stir tribal hatred that had been holding on for years. Just like water that had been contained in a pot on continuous heat, the steam broke loose and erupted from the lid. What later escalated was bloodshed, which cost our great nation its once famed peace—*talk about the land of peace, love, and unity.* All that was thrown into the trash. Our country was no more than a wasteland of savages, who went to the point of setting ablaze a church with congregants in it.

I tried hard to forget about the deaths way back. They had caused me sleepless nights when I was still in my early teens. What fueled my anger more was hearing Christian people give testimonies of how they survived amid the deaths that ravaged the others. I wondered why they would glorify survival, they were no different from the Darwinists. I watched the road wind up several hills to Ressentir county. It was green and full of life. I had finally gotten a view of the place. Considering how long our journey was, I wondered how the white men had mapped and administered our country to its farthest reaches.

One of the greatest highlights of 21st-century technology was the digitization of maps. In my time, whenever I would get lost, I would refer to virtual assistants, in turn, they would give me visual feedback on my location and provide further directions. Since Jacques was in dire need of honoring a promise to his daughter—*buying her hot peri peri pizza,* I quickly referred to my Google Assistant for further help. We were about twenty miles from Ressentir town. The assistant notified us that there were no pizzerias around the place.

The landscape was made of hills everywhere. The roads were narrow and full of winding. Étienne had commented that the end of Kenyane civilization would reach its prophetic fulfillment at the end of that town. True to his words, my cell service reception started getting weaker, while the infrastructural glory faded away with every passing every mile. I was content with an area not having proper roads and fancy buildings; the thing I never wanted messed with was my internet connection, which was

23

technically a part of my lifeline. As a generation Z, my tech-savvy nature wouldn't allow for that.

I remembered a while back in Naroque. After witnessing the reckless driver being pulled over, we had taken a short drive and then pulled over next a grocery seller. The trend of roadside trade was very common along the Kenyane roads. The road was sandy but full of shrubs and thickets. After opening my door, I walked elegantly as if sampling a newer world like the early explorers. My experience was akin to Neil Armstrong when he first set foot on the moon. The only difference between him and I was that I was not in a space-suit. After taking a short leak, I joined in the rest and helped them pack groceries. They bought the following items: a bucketful of potatoes, three pounds of carrots, and loads of onions.

Ressentir town was however different. Most of the buildings were literally on higher ground. The place where we parked our car was at the center of a hill. Since there was no pizza, we had to do what every sensible human would do, we bought a cake. Jacques was okay with us adding our shopping items to his tab, but I felt less morally obligated to do that. I bought myself a pack of M&Ms, chocolate bars, and a smoothie. We were an hour away from our destination. So, I felt my impatience slowly drift away. We took a brief walk around the mall we were in. It was not long before Jacques and I said we wanted to go to the washrooms, all at the same time. It felt kind of weird, but whatever, we were dudes.

I had had some experience using lavish washrooms. My days as a volunteer had paid off. The school director had become fond of my English, and French-speaking skills. That had made me capable of interacting with any well-wishers who came to visit his school. He also loved my non-self-centeredness. I didn't go about asking for money from the visitors. That is why they took me as their designated guide to all their trips and cruises around town. That got me exclusive access to luxury shopping malls and other high-end places around the city. Whenever people saw me with them, they assumed that I hailed from a high-end family, I felt a little ashamed of that. Knowing too well that in the end, after the day's activities, I would be retiring at the slums. The Kenyane film, *La Vie Demi du Naïrobi*, started to make some sense to me.

I went to the lavatories and helped myself for a brief period, which I didn't want to end. The air freshener smelled with an appeal which caught my nasal faculties. At the end of the room, where I was in, were baby wipes. It felt a little gay to use them; but in as much as people had senseless stereotypes about other people's sexual orientations, I dismissed that gibberish as absolute nonsense and helped myself to one of them. The wipes were soaked in a strong alcoholic concoction, which made my skin have a burning feel—*in the most pleasant way.*

"Hey, Reveur! Why are you marooning yourself in the toilet? Man, you need to … forget it,"

"Coming Jacques. Give me a minute, it seems that the lack of fiber in my diet isn't doing me a solid. Everything is stuck down here, oh!"

We left and found Étienne in the electronics section of the mall. I found it a bit weird for a grown man to go around window shopping and taking snapshots of every item that came in their way. He, however, seemed fine by his actions. We tagged along with him for about five minutes before we got to the car and headed for Moustique town. The weather was starting to get a little chilly. I predicted there would be rain in the afternoon.

Jacques had a strong love for his mother. He told us that he would always call his mother whenever he had reached Ressentir town. She would later prepare him the lunch of a king. I envied the love he had for his mother. When he called her, she said she was not around, his only option was to redirect the task to his sister, who was more than happy to take over the task. From the way they talked, I sensed a strong platonic bond within them.

Immediately we had left Ressentir land, the roads started getting messier. I wondered how in the world that had happened. The government usually allocated billions in cash for individual county development, but it seemed that the Lac counties were keen on politicking than on positive development. It made little sense that the regions nearer to Naïrobi had world class development, but the closer to the edge of the country, everything was all different. Some people had said that on taking off, a ride on a plane was very bumpy, it was similar to our experience on that road. The bumpiness and roughness of the road created some rhythm which my body was trying to get in sync with. To make it worse, the dust around was enveloping the whole surrounding owing to the many vehicles moving around.

There were huge tractors and heavy trucks around the road. The many plant operating machines and road detours suggested that the road was under construction. It was a huge stretch of road of about fifty miles. According to my calculations, it would take about a year or more for the project to finish. For several miles, they had dug about fifteen feet of the road and filled it with layers of hard sedimentary rock. I liked the fact that they had flattened it, so it was good to go for the vehicles. The only problem was the rocks that fell off the trucks ferrying them—*they made navigation a living hell*. Since Jacques's car had a chassis closer to the ground, we could hear its impact with any stray rocks we passed.

I saw several Chinese workers wearing their straw hats and smoking from their pipes. It was fun watching them supervise the local workers; they spoke in a made-up pidgin consisting of Mandarin, broken Swahili, and English. I laughed myself off when one of the workers just nodded his head in agreement. He hadn't heard anything but still made an effort to show his comprehension. Jacques picked his phone and changed the playlist. We had listened to old school hits for a while, it was time for the new generation pop. Despite being six years older, he claimed his taste in music was influenced by his maturity, as opposed to mine. I took it as an offense and then bit my lip in rage.

We passed Mensonge township, if it were to be nominated for its beauty, then it would grace the wall of shame. It had only one street with dilapidated buildings. There was nothing worth seeing there, and the only good thing about it was its road. It was a single lane, one which was suffering the fate of Sino-construction. We didn't even make a stop at that place. There was a slight difference in the landscape as we moved further away from Ressentirland, there were more hills and numerous rocks. To say that the land was arable would be a lie. Farming existed on tiny packets of farmlands that were graced with 'real' soil. It was a hard thing to spot it around.

A fun fact is the region was originally inhabited by Nilo-Saharan peoples. Their prior economic activities were pastoralism and fishing. However, when the Bantu—*the largest African linguistic group*—had their migration kick in, the newbies exploited the opportunity and seized all the farmland they could get. The Maragoli peoples, my kind, were the last to move in there, about two centuries before. Since we were collaborators of colonialism, we were hired in to support the crown administration. And with land up for grabs, we were able to buy it cheaply and also call in our relatives from the western region. Fast-forwarding to the present, our numbers had increased and we claimed we owned the place.

My solitude at the back of the car threw me again into my old memories. Félicité was a good girl. After knowing her for a while during my vacation, I felt the urge to brag to the world she was mine. Most of my peers and my television experience had taught me to always propose to a lady. I was slightly older than her, so I knew I had some advantage. We always met in the mornings when she was taking milk to the dairy and later in the afternoon when she would be taking her family's cattle to the river. In all our meeting sessions, I made every effort to prolong our time as possible. I had never known the love of a woman before, but whatever she shared with me was truly special. I had made fun of people who said they were in love, but when I had finally gotten a sip of the juice, things started getting different—*the succulence was addictive.*

That night when I had escorted her to her place and then walked in the dark, my aunt was furious. She was up and running about my irresponsibility and carelessness. Her main argument was that my teenage rebellion had taken over. She cried about how I was an angel before puberty had kicked in. My lack of interest in her pointless nagging prompted me to stand back and act dumb. After a while, she asked me to help her clean up. My elder sister, who babysat her, was away on a trip. I was left with the responsibility of her caregiving. She had been suffering from a stroke ever since I could remember. I felt pity for her every-time I looked into her eyes. Beneath her tough-lady face was an innocent young girl, who was scared of her condition.

It took me guts but I finally proposed to her. Félicité was a bit old school. A week of being around her had already gotten me to second base. We were past hand-holding, and I had moved on to holding the waist and light kissing. I had no idea how to kiss a lady, but my experience had come from years of watching Telenovelas. The stage was set near her gate at exactly seven in the evening. That day had been a Saturday. After taking her to church, we went to town and grabbed a pizza large and a cola. It was too much for us to finish, we had to carry the leftovers. I had an advantage on the terrain. There were many hills, so very little people made an effort to take commercial cars to our place from town. We had to walk. I took that opportunity to talk to her about everything. Amid the trees and no passers-by, I held on to her waist and felt the rhythm of her bodily movements, while trying to get into sync with her breathing. The walk was long but we finally came close to her house.

As we approached her house, it was already getting dark. I had packaged a gift for her. It was a pack of sanitary pads sealed with ribbon. I had read online on how to gift a lady one loved, and that was the only thing my naivety could pick. After giving it to her, I stretched out my hands and held on to her waist. Her days hanging out with me had taught her to be as free as possible with me. She looked away briefly and then smiled. Her eyes were locked on my tiny waist. She was slightly bigger than me in terms of body size, but her argument was that she liked my physique because of the many advantages it posed. I didn't want to know what they were.

A Daunting Jaunt

After leaning in for a kiss, she looked away and then let go off me. I felt overly alarmed but then moved on gently to hold her hands. Her eyes had that spark which I had never seen anywhere else. She was the kind of woman who would make a guy go mad. She hinted out that it was getting late. Within that instant I felt the magic words coming out of me, 'Could you be my girlfriend ...' They didn't come out clearly, but I saw her leave without saying a word. It felt very strange to me. I had no option but to leave. Knowing too well that my stay out there was coming to an end, I braced myself for the worst. I prayed hard that I would appease Calliope, in the hope that her infinite wisdom would grant me the power to compose a verse, which would sweep my girl off her feet.

Jacques was keen on looking at me with his rearview mirror. He smiled hard when he saw me dozing off. My eyes were red like that of a junkie. He was happy I was no drug abuser, if so, he said, I would have been the worst. I congratulated him for the compliment, while I openly frowned upon. The road from Mensonge had been smooth, but when we had neared Aller, the home of the Sony Sugar Company, things started getting from better to worse. It was like witnessing in live-action, a problematic period. The road had cracks all over and gigantic potholes. After a ten-mile stretch from the sugar company, we were met with the mother of all Kenyane potholes. It covered a diameter almost the size of the road, and a length of about five meters. We had to drive on the sidewalk—*which was non-existent by the way.* It was a dangerous choice since a truck had overturned just because of that, but we had no other alternative.

There were lots of sugar plantations all over. I had mistaken the sugar cane for Napier grass. The dudes laughed at me hard, I joined in their joke just to piss them off. Since we were driving in a posh car and wore decent clothes, the locals looked at us with aspirations. They assumed we were Naïrobien tourists out there ready to help them. After what we seemed like a Savannah safari, in the colonial days, my phone assistant signaled we were a few kilometers to Moustique town. Jacques made a detour using the Caverne de Buffle road. We didn't get to see the town itself. The only thing that was interesting was my sleeping all the way. I got easily bored with the tiny farms and the dusty road. We made a few turns and were finally home. The weather was already changing. The clouds were gray and ready to explode their wombs.

I had been to that place a decade before, back when Jacques was still broke and in college. I had gone there to seek asylum. After missing school for almost a year for lack of fees, I had requested my cousin to take me to the land of my father. If I were in the States, I guess I would have written something about it, maybe I would have been elected into the presidency. At that time there was zero development. The roads were a mess. But later then, things had changed and I felt proud to be witnessing them. Jacques had constructed a huge mansion for his wife, and a smaller one for his mother. I started beating myself up for not being able to do the same. I didn't want to live in the lie that things would turn out better for me; my youngest uncle had thought of that, but where was he at that moment?

From a distance, I could see his house had a red-tiled roof, with a fresh plastering. It had metallic doors and window grills. It was truly remarkable. On the contrary, his mother's had green tiles, it lay adjacent to the gate entrance, while the other stood in the opposite far end. The gate was made of rusty iron sheets, perhaps because the place was still under construction—*but I highly doubted that.* There was an acacia tree at the center of the compound. It was fully green and a little shorter than the ones I had seen in the drylands. We parked the car and opened its doors, Jacques ordered us to leave them open—*he wanted the neighbors to know he had arrived.* He played Dholuo music, from the tribe where Barrack Obama's father hailed, and then took out a bottle of whiskey from his car dashboard. I knew he would act all drunk in a few minutes. At that moment, I took out my phone and started taking snapshots of the place.

We were welcomed by Jacques's sister, Jacqueline. She stood about five feet five inches, about a foot shorter than her brother. She gave him a hug and then waved at me and Étienne. She gestured to us where we would place our stuff and then after making sure we were back from the house, gave us a tour around Jacques's house, it was still under construction. The craftsmen were doing the final touches, in an effort to make the house habitable within a few months. A quick inspection in the inside revealed its sheer size and magnificence. It had many hallways and countless rooms. As a man who was in love with culinary practices, I was especially amazed by the fact that the house had two modern kitchens. I looked at myself in awe as I remembered the size of my kitchen back at home, it was a makeshift space in the middle of my mother's single-room house. I took several photos of the place as we toured around. After finishing Jacqueline's short tour, she directed us to her mother's house. It was slightly smaller but was packed with excellent furniture. It was by far better than my dad's. I quickly felt at home there, and immediately fell into a deep sleep at that moment. I left Jacques sorting through the stuff he had bought along the way. It seemed like he was selecting some for his wife, who was living in town, and some for his mother.

Once in my sleep, I didn't see much as in my previous dream. I saw myself in a chamber. The light was very bright white. I felt blinded by it since most of it was aiming for my eyes. I looked around and noticed I was all alone. In front of me was a blue door with a black curtain. At the side of the door were two jerrycans; the window was wooden and creaky, I could see gaping holes in the walls. At the center was a rusty old table. Perhaps, my subconscious had a loving for the chubby chic décor. I felt an urge to scream and shout in despair. Maybe, that would awaken whoever was bound to save me. As I approached to open the door, I noticed it was not a door at all, everything had vanished and I was in an infinite space of whiteness. Above me was a white misty covering, which I lacked any comprehension of.

"Hey, Maman, Nuit, and Réveiller, what have you done? You have sat on my daughter's cake. What have you done?"

I was awoken from my slumber by Jacques's noisiness. He was very loud. I had earlier rested on a two-seat couch. It was a bit uncomfortable, I had to raise my legs from my knee caps. Jacqueline had given me two cushions, one for the legs and the other for my head. I woke up in full confusion. My mouth was filled with saliva, while my eyes were still sleepy. He continued about how the cake had been ruined after the three girls had accidentally dropped it, probably after fighting for it. It was hilarious and I felt like laughing a little—*I had to put on a serious face lest I be a victim of circumstance.* He walked there and there until he retired to a seat due to exhaustion.

His sister had been diligent enough to make sure a fine meal was ready for us. She prepared a buffet of *xima—cooked corn flour, sardines, and green peas.* And to my delight, the meal was accompanied by a cup of water. I couldn't be any happier. Despite most of my hosts offering to say the grace before meals, I generally preferred to make a sign of the cross and dive into the meal ASAP. Étienne was quick to gobble up his portion and ask for more. Jacques looked at him in surprise and assured that everything was on a self-service basis. We all laughed at his remark. Funny thing though was our hosts opted not to dine with us. If it were a strange place, I would fear my food was poisoned.

After having a hearty meal, one that I ate only for the fill and not the delicacy, Jacques called us together to the sitting room. Little did I know that it had rained for like an hour while I was asleep. It was super muddy in the outside. The floor tiles we had carried had already been arranged at the dining chamber. They lay next to a makeshift study room for Jacqueline's three daughters. As a lover of readership, I was especially moved by their enthusiasm. The tiles had caused much trouble when we had left Naïrobi. Étienne had thought he was the clever one. After repeatedly telling him to space them at the back of the car, he ignored my request. However, when Jacques came over he quickly undid the former's works and spaced them out evenly. I agreed with his actions considering we had just replaced the car's shocks the previous day.

The study had high school and religious literature. I simply looked at them and flipped through some pages. I felt less compelled to indulge myself in reading. There was a unique feeling that came along with that place, Moustique, the weather was equatorial and desert-like. I felt a slight warm breeze and then a chilly one. Right when I had left the city, I knew I would crash at his house. Upon hearing his it was unfinished and that his wife was living at a rented bungalow downtown, I was thrilled about the idea of living there. Sadly, he hit me with news that I would be staying up in the village. 'Man,' I said to myself in disappointment. Up there was no good. I dismissed my earlier zeal for staying upcountry. He would instead be going with Étienne to his house, one with more than enough rooms to host me and a dozen guys—*assuming we were to squeeze in.* I had no other alternative. I had to stay there. He promised he would be coming during the day and we would be having countless road-trips, I knew that was a lie. Knowing him too well, I would have to find pleasant co-curricular activities, otherwise, I would be crying to myself.

I had been away from that place for a decade. The people I knew then were either away or dead. The ones that were left were either too busy to have any care for me or unmoved by the return of a prodigal guest. I stood with a fake smile as the car zoomed away from the homestead. It was one heck of an experience I would rather have not happened to me. The three girls were more than happy to have me around. They called me uncle frequently, despite my preference for my name. They were the kind of people who still held on to the long lost values of respect, honor, and obedience. My earlier turmoil and anger started to slowly fade away—*time did heal scars.*

I wondered why Nuit and Réveiller would even think of considering me their elder. I was within their age group range, a bit older, but not that much. To me, the word uncle carried a lot of meaning. I saw no point in people throwing it around just like that. Of the two, Nuit seemed more of the mature kind. I felt moved to converse with her. I tried hard not to be too open to her. The last thing I wanted was opening up my problematic life story to my niece. It would be a bit too unconventional.

With several hours ahead until the night kicked in, I decided to give my cousin, Ardente a visit. He had lived with me way back at my family's Nakŭru home. His stay over there had lasted for a year. So, the amount of time I had spent with him was that which I was on vacation from school. He had been a good guy. I had especially learned something important from him, I needed to stand up for myself. Previously, back when I was I primary school, I had suffered abuse from my elder brothers—*getting beaten up senselessly.*

Right from the start, after my father had had a fatal accident, he had no other option but to send me to the Nakŭru home. I studied from my fifth to the eighth year of primary school over there. His wives had deserted him, so, the option was to place me under the care of my elder brothers. As a ten year old, I was very weak and frail, my shorter stature had dealt a huge blow on me. I was the object of daily whupping. I would do all the household chores while in tears. In my sixth year, I decided enough was enough. I went over to stay at our neighbor's house for about three months. What followed were rotations around my school teachers' houses. By the time I was in my seventh year, my father brought in a lady, Joanne, who stayed with me. For the very least, she was the one who protected me from my brother's and taught me the Maragoli language, my native tongue.

I was a very bright student, so the abuses never deterred me in any way from working hard. After joining high school, I started living with my father's other wife in the city, I was at least away

from the abuse. However, whenever I visited, I was no exception.
With Joanne gone away on some trip, I got the better of their
beatings. It was until Ardente had come that we started fighting
off the brutal brothers. I was sixteen by then and a little taller. He
even taught me martial arts. After getting fed up with my home,
he took up all his savings and invited me on a trip of a lifetime, a
visit to my father's home, which was his home too. We had
traveled to find two funerals awaiting us. Both my aunts had lost
their sons. The causes of the deaths were in everyone's lips.
Murmurs around suggested they had died of HIV. They had
thought themselves too brave to take anti-retroviral medication,
they had learned the hard way so it seemed.

Ardente was my age mate. I was four months older though.
Albeit his 'not seeing anything in school—*a local expression for F
students*', he had successfully managed to quit school at the
primary level, impregnate an underage girl—*who he was forced to
marry by the way, and wait for it ..., construct single-handedly a mud-walled
house with corrugated iron sheets*. It was a good thing he was forced to
take care of the poor girl. He worked around like a metal welding
artisan. He prided himself in having made the metal grills that
held Jacques's house windows. Jacques had told me earlier, that
he had paid him a thousand dollars for the task.

He still lived in his father's homestead. It was slightly different
from the way I had left it earlier. There was a footpath that lay
adjacent to the top right of their land. It was about a meter wide,
it stretched several yards to their main gate, I had to make a left
turn to get in. Next to the gate was a water well, and to the left
was his house. In the far right was his brother, Nuée's house. It
had the same architectural style. Next to their houses were their
mothers', the only difference was that they were twice bigger. I
took a look at his wife, who was standing at his door. She was a

bit shorter than me but lighter in the skin. Her hair was radiant, perhaps because of the never-ending visits to her coiffeur's place.

At first glance, she wondered who I was. Her super googly eyes were redirected at me. I moved forward to greet her. I was used to hugging ladies whenever I was saying hi, but since I was in foreign territory, I had no other alternative but to play it cool. I guessed maybe Ardente must have been resting after a tiresome day of work. However, the moment he heard my voice, he was up and running from the house. It took me a while to guess who he was. Quite frankly, the only thing I could recognize from him was his voice, everything else was blurry. I would bet that a proper nickname for him could have been Scar-face. He had many scars and an aged facial structure. Whoever said that poverty made someone look older than themselves wasn't that wrong after all.

"Brother, how are you? It's been a long time. Man, you never age at all. Your baby-like face is still there, you have no beard and a good thing, you're slightly shorter than me. I had warned you earlier bro, there is no way you will ever get any taller than me,"

"Oh, I've taken note of that."

He sensed the little resentment I had from the way I responded to his 'victory speech', he led me into the house and then asked his wife to bring in a flask of hot tea. As a guy who had lived with me for a longer period, he knew the only thing that would cool me was a cup of hot tea. After many years of trying to understand myself, I later learned I was bipolar. I used to wonder how I would go from being cheerful to being all silent and depressed. It used to affect my social life, and it cost me my relationships with eligible bachelorettes. I used to beat myself up about that, but I had learned to deal with all that. The solution was being a loner.

At least, I didn't hurt anyone else except for myself.

His house had two rooms. The bedroom was hidden from plain sight, the only view that I got to sample was the living room. It was composed of a round table—*that reminded me of King Arthur, his knights, and the Excalibur, and four plastic seats.* The walls were covered in huge posters of reggae artists and Box Office movie stars. I could see images of Cynthia Rothrock, Van Damme, Jackie Chan, … I lost interest in guessing who the stars were in the reggae legends section. I was served with three cups of chai tea. If I were at a coffee shop in Naïrobi, I would have ordered for a chai-latte, but well, … things don't work out as we hope them to.

His talk revolved around our time back when I last visited his place. I had attended several dances during that time. The only problem for me at the time was my lack of comprehension for the local vernacular. That had denied me the chance to hook up with the girls. They said my Swahili was full of slang, and my English was way overboard. I had an unknown dislike for the local languages, so I made no effort in learning them. After about a month and a half, I had managed to make friends with only one girl. She liked the fact that I was a walking opportunity for her to perfect her spoken English. I even went on ahead to teach her Français and some Espagnol.

As I took a final sip, Ardente narrated to me how the girl was married with kids, and how she was dying to meet me one final time. Knowing that I had taught her languages to the best of my ability, I felt a little infuriated all that had gone to waste. I forced a smile and suggested we take a walk around town. Since the rain had hit hard, it was very muddy. Any attempt walking to town would be an all-out disaster. He offered to lend me his mother's boots, they were unisex, so I had no fear of being labeled 'a transvestite'. I thanked his wife for the nice tea before we left.

As we walked, I lost count of whatever we were talking about. My mind was drifting to my earlier love life. We had passed several homesteads and walked downhill to town, we noticed that a fast-moving car would have overturned had the road not been winding. I remembered when Félicité had not responded to my proposal. I had left for school after the holidays had come to a close. She had gone AWOL after that night. After several days of not seeing her, I packed my bags and headed to school. She was the subject of my daily chats with my friends at school. Most of my friends said she had zero interest in me, and that I should hit the road. I took no heed of their advice. I simply let whatever they said to vanish into a thin air of nothingness.

After a year, I later returned to our Naküru home. I went there with high hopes. I had never gotten laid with a girl before, I had preserved that moment for her alone. It didn't matter if she decided it to be when we had finished school or whatever, I was down for anything. I had composed and memorized several poems for her. With two limericks, three free verses, and four haiku's in her honor, I knew she would be on top of the world when she listened to my recitations.

My elder brother, the black sheep, was notorious for beating me up and causing trouble at home. When I got home, he showed little respect to me. Ardente and I had taught him a lesson. The homestead had two houses with four rooms for the boys, and a gigantic one at the center for the boys. My house was adjacent to his. I hadn't announced my homecoming yet. So, he had no idea I was coming there yet. I had joined the martial arts club at school, so I was ready for any fall-outs with him.

I quietly opened the gate. It didn't make its usual creaky noise. Perhaps, it had been recently oiled at its hinges. The grass was greenish-yellow, owing to the prevalent dry season, I expected the worse to happen. It was a good thing the place never got desert dry. As I walked nearer, I heard a familiar lady voice coming from his room. He had not cared to close the door. Due to the sparse population, no one ever bothered to unexpectedly enter one's home. I stealthily crept closer to his room; I was eager to quench my curiosity—*I hoped no cat would get killed in the process, I did love kitties.*

His door was ajar, I stood with my mouth agape when I saw what was before my eyes. Félicité was lying on his bed with him. Her hair was a bit messy, and she had a bed sheet covering her glory. Tears rolled down my eyes as I walked away. She seemed to care less about my heartbreak. My brother looked at me in triumph as he smiled. He gave me the look of satisfaction as I was reaching a point of total devastation. It wouldn't take long before my bipolar episodes would begin. She unashamedly got dressed and left our home. She swung her body while walking, as if in mockery of me.

Ardente had been busy talking to a dumb recipient. He talked with great command. I had a different accent from the locals. I never spoke the local lingo, so he felt proud that he could throw in a mix of Swahili in our conversations. I also looked a little exotic. I had different physical features from the people around; first, my hair was less kinky, softer, and curlier. Second, I had lighter and somehow reddish-brown skin. The guys around with skin similar to mine had different hair, which sold them out.

We walked a few minutes and reached his dad's rental settlement. There were less than ten houses under occupation, the rest were either still under development, or were delegated as convenience stores. We walked into their 'gold mine'. The occupants of the houses were not very friendly. They passed us by without the usual 'hi' that always popped up whenever one came across newer people in their midst. I felt less obliged to care about that. Outside that place were crossroads. Four roads connected from all over, and at the epicenter was Jacques's house, several scores of meters away. Due to the latter's 'bad heart,' we chose to walk to town than 'hear it' from him.

Ardente told me the place was called En Descendant, it lay in close, *à proximité,* to the administrative area of the region. Considering Moustique was a county, all the major offices were located there. I was impressed by the sheer beauty of the government offices. Next to them were the old colonial houses. It amazed me further how they had survived for more than a century without any need for renovation. Aside from the usual paint jobs and electrical fitting, the houses had stood the tests of time. Funny enough, they all stood on a hill. It seemed the white folks never wanted anything to do with flooding. The place had gotten its weird name from the expression, *piqure de moustique,* a constant mosquito bite. The tropical climate and the dampness in many parts of the area all affirmed that statement.

What I liked the most about that place was the ladies. I was used to living with and dating ladies from around the Naïrobi region, and if I went further enough I would go for Naküru—*No offense intended, but the ladies over there were not that endowed when it came to the posteriors.* I wasn't talking about the fat lady ones, no, a slim figure girl who was well endowed. They were all over the place in Moustique town. Some would say I wasn't far into the reach of perversion. I tried hard to hide that fact. There were lots of reckless motorcycle riders. I almost got crashed into while focusing deeply into some lady's bodily swings.

Ardente was all over about young girls in the area making blunt out excuses to their parents, whenever a dance was about to take place in town, they called it *dansant*, they would lie about some church event they were going to. Armed with their lady charms and sweet talks, their parents would have no other option but to give in. I had been full of shenanigans during my time, that, however, was beyond me. I had found a group out of my league.

We toured the town for about an hour. It was almost getting dark, and from the look that Ardente gave me, I knew he wanted a tip or something for his good work done. He was an alcoholic, so he expected me to take him to some bar and spoil him. As a strict nonalcoholic, I did what every sensible rationalist would do, I bought him: milk, sugar, tea-leaves, and cookies. He had a five-year-old kid, a by-product of his earlier illicit sexual adventure, who I reckoned would love my gifts. We hurriedly left town and headed for his home. It took us an hour by foot to get there. My earlier eight-hour travel coupled up with several hours walk to town was enough to make me fatigued beyond mention.

We got to Ardente's home, his mother was away on a funeral, his wife and kid were watching a sitcom, called Jeune Personne. It was a story about the protagonist, Cadet, and his family living out in the *Les terres de Naïrobi est*. There was also a guy working for them from the Luhya community, my tribe belonged to it. There was always a stereotype that my people loved eating lots of food—*that was what was portrayed in that program*. I detested it for that. But it got better when I started following the story.

The boy had gotten fed up of school. All he wanted to do was to join in on what his fellow peers were into—*making money*. After a lengthy quarrel with his granny, he did what every other sensible kid would do. He opted to figure out life on his own. However, after a day of no luck in his job-hunting mission; he was all bending-knees back to his home. Life was no joke out there. There was some air of zero tranquility in his house, the Luhya guy was mad that the food rations would be reduced.

After watching it for about ten minutes, I got bored. I took my phone and started browsing the internet. There was nothing special online in social media. My Facebook and Twitter accounts were buzzing with crappy memes. I had to literally laugh out loud at the funny comments people had come up with. Everyone in the room, Ardente, his wife, his kid, and his brother, all looked at me in disbelief. I signaled them to 'not' mind whatever I had done. They continued getting glued to the TV screen. They were indeed television zombies.

I continued surfing the web. My thumb was my surfboard. I had recently joined an online community targeted at polishing my rusty French. It had been about three months, and I spoke like a real francophone. I had earlier been subjected to criticism by a group of Congolese nationals, I had been working with. They had argued that I was faking a Parisian accent, I simply laughed at their complement. Theirs was however off the charts, like crazy badly pronounced French. It took me a while to realize that food had already been served on the table.

As a rule, any guest would open the field for munching by being the first to wash their hands. Ardente's wife, Dorcasse, stood in front of me with a large blue bowl full of water. I looked at her in pity. As a staunch believer of the feminist cause, I was against male chauvinistic ideals. She basically did most of the house,

farm, and everything work. It seemed unfair that she had to
shoulder all that burden while all the male members of the house
just stood by and watched. I had no other alternative but to
accept her act of hospitality. After subjecting my hands to a
rigorous cleaning experience, I felt kind of elated.

The meal was composed of *xima* and sardines, I wondered why
folks around that place liked it that much. When I came to think
of it, the meal was ginormous, it was fit for *une douzaine de
personnes*. I lacked the courage to say I wouldn't eat much. They
were all over me about how I should eat well. And by well, they
meant eating like it was my last. I took my final chunk of *xima*
and washed my hands hastily. It looked dark, and with most hot
regions, snakes were bound to be roaming around. I bid them
farewell quickly and then promised Ardente to return the boots
he had lent me.

The road to Jacques's home was brilliantly dark. With no
moonlight to shine up my way, I used my phone for that
purpose. On my left was a huge church, called *Les Derniers en
Appelant*, it was an asylum for the mentally deranged, and
religious psychos. From a distance, it looked like a school
playground. There was a main building at the center, built like an
unconventional church-house, and the rest were smaller houses,
about nine square feet each. My small sightseeing finally ended
after I unexpectedly bumped into Jacques's mother, Béatrice,
who wore a black dress. In her hand was a small handbag. She
didn't recognize me at first. Having grown taller and more
muscular than before, she got lost for a moment before
recollecting who I was.

Next to her newly constructed house was her former one, now
turned into a kitchen. We walked into it and found both

Jacqueline and her three daughters. The house had an empty room at the entrance and after it, one that was the dining table— I wondered why they wouldn't simply use the modern and more elegant one in the new house, it even had a kitchen compartment *(talk of people still in the old times)*. I had learned before that to make new friends at a new place, one had to show no fear. I tried hard to blend in quickly. I remembered those kids from earlier in the day. They all smiled at me and then asked for my phone. They were all turned up by the idea of virtual assistants, luckily, my phone had the exact tool they needed. They laughed at the wonders modern technology could do. It was fine guiding them through the whole process.

The table was filled with xima and meat. For every village family, having a guest over required cooking something special. To them, that was it. I felt a bit offended that my worth was reduced to all that. Considering that I had eaten at my cousin's place, adding something extra in my system would have been overkill. They however insisted and that got the better of me. In spite of them filling my plate with zeal, I disappointed them by delving into it only halfway. The girls seemed to have an appetite. Maman was especially full of it, she was the cheeky one. I liked her for that.

The night was young and full of life. We spent most of it discussing my father's early childhood days. In a way, I got to understand the root cause of his current lifestyle and choices. Most of their talk was full of exaggeration, but I went along with whatever they said. Several narrations by Jacqueline told me she was not for real—she was barely born when my dad was a teenager, and her mom was a youngish girl who knew little about him. I got bored with their talk. It was full of selfish exaltation, about how they were poor before, and how they were now 'rich'. I learned much from their primitive talk. It got me into a mode, where I played dumb and focused not on what they said, but only on my self-reflections.

My mind started racing back to memory lane. After about a year away from my Nakŭru home, I had decided to go back and rekindle old memories. I had become heartbroken, but I felt like I owed it to myself to see Félicité once more. It felt a bit weird when I came to think of it. I had no idea how I would approach her. Most of the time when I closed school for the holidays, I preferred going to Naïrobi. But at that moment I headed for that place. There was nothing new about it. All seemed as boring as ever.

My nemesis of a brother was away at that time. That provided an opening for me to confront the girl. There was no brilliance in her innocence. All that had faded after she had learned about 'men'. I got the word around that she was hooking up with every John and Doe. I got a little mad, but all that was ill-directed emotion. It was meant to be placed elsewhere. I wondered what the hell was wrong with me; there were countless girls around, but I chose to stick to a pile of jinx.

After getting home, I settled down finally. Félicité's family had finally moved next to our place—It was like having your neighbor watch another episode of the *Le jeu des trônes* on cable, you detest it, but you have no other option, since your cable subscription was cut, well … spoilers! Every morning I got myself a treat of a lifetime. She would walk past our compound, probably her shortcut, while she acted like I was non-existent. I tried to ignore for a while, but enough was enough. Albeit her inconsideration, I felt morally inclined to ask her something. And also, I was a bit infatuated with her.

"Hey Reveur, time to sleep. It seems the journey to this place has done quite a number on you,"

I looked at Jacqueline as she held a hurricane lamp, a bucket of water and a towel. I knew for a second, sleep was not the thing she was asking for. She gave them hurriedly to me and signaled to me the path to the bathroom. I claimed that I was a macho man, but the upcountry darkness was sending me the chills. Next to Jacques's mother's house was a bathroom, a few yards away from the back door. It was a nicely constructed structure. A brick-walled *le salle de bain* with two rooms for the showers and two for the toilets. The latter were less fancy—pit latrines, uh! I walked in and got myself the shower of a lifetime.

I knew that in most situations, the folks upcountry would treat you like a king, but if you stayed for more than a week, things would start getting a bit less funky. The water was super hot. I cleaned up and then washed my boxer shorts. There was a mini clothing line inside there, so I hung my shorts and socks, they were torn at the heels—but I cared less. If anyone were to ask, I was just being too much of a man to care.

After cleaning up and feeling overly refreshed, I took to the kitchen where I found Réveiller and Nuit. They were overly happy to see me. After their meals, they headed to their makeshift study—*floor tiles were piled all over*. I was impressed to showcase my arithmetic and grammatical skills. They all felt elated for the wonderful performance I had given them. I was ready for an encore, but their mother kept pestering them to sleep. Maman had left with Béatrice to her room. Nuit, her mother, and her sister led me to a small cottage-like house in the outside. It belonged to Jacques's older brother. They were all for taking care of it, lest the rats and snakes made it their permanent residence.

At first, I had thought they would take me to the house and leave me there. I could swear I would've screamed if I were to spend a single night there, alone. It was pitch dark and cold like outer space, but when Jacqueline said, 'Let me bring in light ...', the place looked splendid. It was a single room with three compartments; two-sheet fabrics separated the sitting room from the two-bed sections. There was a table at the center, and two two-person-couches on either side. I was a very sleepy, so I stood by the door and awaited orders from the lady. I was ready to do what she said. After all, like a student, I was under her care for the next seven days or so.

"Hey, Reveur, please take the bed in the far left from the door. I will be sleeping with Réveiller, and Nuit will be taking the couch. Okay, please sleep tight, *bonne nuit*,"

«*À demain ,*»

I responded to her goodnight with a 'see you tomorrow'. She fell on her bed with a huge thud. The two girls read for an hour until Réveiller succumbed to the sweet calling of sleep. I was left with Nuit. Having a younger person with me gave me the opportunity to whisper in a few words of wisdom. I talked to her for a moment, but it didn't take long before I finally dozed off. She was busy with her reading, I never did realize when she took to her sleep.

Everyone's talk about how Jacques had finally succeeded got me into a temporal zone of fantasy. Like a keen student researcher of theoretical physics, I felt as if my mind was in constant immersion into a singularity of nothingness, later, my life unfolded after a huge bang—*the big bang*. In what seemed like a pandemonium breaking loose, the sheer confusion gave rise to things like my consciousness and emotional faculties. Now, they were all drifting apart from each other. I couldn't feel myself, what was left was only a loose conception of it.

In my dreams, I saw myself driving a car. It was a state of the art Peugeot design, midnight-black and with wicked rims. I assumed it came from Paris. As an *assimilé*, everything French was a turn on. I flashed it everywhere for all to see. Upon closer inspection, I saw myself as not being any different from Jacques, and what I hated about him. With me was a beautiful white lady, my wife, and our children, who spoke excellent French. Since the people around had no idea how to converse in French, I did so with my kids, and they did it well. All were amazed at my luck in scoring a white woman. I walked with her in pride.

A Daunting Jaunt

It was day one upcountry, and I already felt bored. There was no systematic order in that place. People would wake up, take their breakfast, graze their animals, and go to the farmlands. With boring algorithms governing their lives, they all felt content. I frowned upon them in disappointment. I had woken up at around eight. To my surprise, everyone was up. The girls were busy sweeping the compound. Granny, on the other hand, was busy on her broom as always. Jacqueline had gone to work. She managed a small tailoring shop in town. That was where she got something little to supplement whatever allowances Jacques gave them. In a way, I stopped resenting him. He had done a great job of providing for his family.

The cycle continued for days. I would wake up, brush my teeth, watch the girls sweep the compound, and act lazy all day long. It was a vicious cycle of meaninglessness. For once, I tried to reason with what the philosophers: Albert Camus and Søren Kierkegaard, had theorized about existential existence—human life was without meaning. If I had been blessed with their intellect, I would have come up with another life-changing philosophical question, or answer.

After taking my breakfast, I headed to Nuée's place. I tried hard to ask why he wasn't around the day before. I wanted everyone around for my homecoming. He simply explained he was with his girl. In his exact words, he was a married man—*but except for any legal union and home*. He was barely twenty and he was rushing into his life head-on. I gave him false encouragement while he took me to his *le salle de sport*. The gym area was very small but handy. There was a forty-pound barbell, and another twenty pound one. I hated the fact that there were no dumbbells and mechanical weights. I had to make do with whatever was around. We worked out for about an hour, and after that, I gulped in a few cups of water. I was almost finished with my session.

At that time, the drama started at the Les Derniers en Appelant church. It was famed for being a mad-house-treatment center. The nutty people were often flogged and prayed for until they got to their sanity. It was a pretty unconventional method, but I championed it for its results. There was a crazy lady who had left the asylum without notice. She was approaching our gate, Ardente's son, Petit, and his sister's son, Sourire, were busy playing within the premises. Nuée was alarmed at that instant. He got hold of my hand and led me to where the lady was. She walked barefoot, had a short dress—*I could swear if she went far into the woods, she would likely be sexually assaulted,* her hair was shaggy and her stocky nature made her a bit frightening.

Like a knight in less shiny armor, a teenage boy came in from the church running. He held in his hand a very long whip. When he got to her, he started talking to her in Dholuo, which *«je n'ai pas compris»*. Their vis à vis felt like pure gibberish. I felt inclined to go and help, but Nuée held me back as we watched the poor lady get whupped by a boy old enough to be her son. She screamed in agony as she had pain inflicted on her. For a second, I could swear I was getting turned on. I had never pictured myself as a sadomasochist before. After an hour of thorough beatings, she calmed down. I had never known pain could bring in a *tranquilité* of sorts. The kids continued playing safely in the fields as if nothing had happened. I wished I could turn back time and become a kid like them too.

I was in luck that they knew Swahili, so I took to talking and playing with them. They were friendly, and within no time, we were the best of friends. Before I knew it, I had already left with them and headed for Jacques's home. The sun was overhead, and

I heard the blaring music from Jacques's car. He had a special
liking for all the kinds of music I hated. I wished I were a
supreme overlord over the earth, everyone would be humming
rock n' roll, pop, and county music tunes. It was too bad for me
that I could never ride on the proverbial horses made of
wishes—*they were just too wild.*

The compound was full of people from around the village. I
never knew people were opportunists, their zeal had however
gotten out of hand. They had heard about the mystery rich village
son's arrival. I could imagine that for the ones engaged, they had
to make detours and turn back to where there was something to
eat. It was a good thing Jacques had brought in all kinds of
snacks, meats, and patisseries just for that special occasion. As I
entered the gate, people were all over. I could count about a
hundred. They were all joyful and full of life; just like action
figures in a Barbie dollhouse. There were two tables next to the
car. They were packed with everything one would desire in a
brunch. Plus, it was an all-out buffet.

I led the kids to the kitchen. I held Sourire by the arms and
pulled Petit by the hand. He felt elated, seeing his father-figure
was guiding him all the way. For once his uncle and unknown
guest had given him recognition among his peers. They were all
apt on knowing what all the fuss was about in the homestead. I
felt slightly inconvenienced by the baby-sitting. I left the kitchen
to join the 'adults' around the table. They were all in chatter;
either speaking Dholuo or Luhya. I felt socially off. The only

alternative was to chat with Étienne. I pretended to like his choice of music, as he expressed his enthusiasm, just to create a rapport with him. He continued until I couldn't take it anymore. I stood up and headed to where Jacques was. As I took a sneak peek to the kitchen direction, I saw his mom give me a stare. I started getting the creeps from her after she had refused to answer my greeting the previous day and instead had given me a stare.

She signaled her son to go to the kitchen, a few minutes later. The visitors were awaiting instructions to take their meal from the host. It was a kind of a tradition for the latter to hold a small prayer before the others savored their meals. Right after everything was done, Jacques informed me that I was needed in the kitchen. I thought maybe it was a short courtesy call and I would be back. However, when I got there I was informed that my place was not with the guests. I was to eat in the kitchen. A plate of rice and *thé sans lait* was brought before me—*thé avec du lait* was a big deal. I thought hard for thirty minutes what that gesture meant before I could take any sip of that humiliation. I was left there all alone. The faint sounds of laughter and jubilation from the outside made me regret deeply of ever accepting the invitation.

The two kids I had earlier come with continued playing outside. Jacques's brother's two sons and a daughter, and his daughter Heureux were all over the place. The latter was afraid of me at first. I tried all the lady charms I knew on her, at three she was a bit difficult. She instead continued to run hither and thither until all the kids around had disappeared. The day before, I had offered to wash my clothes in the morning; Jacqueline instead reprimanded me for my action. It was indeed a crime for a guest to start doing chores in the infancy stage of their visit. I had to oblige. It was Nuit who came to my aid, I was left in amazement at her excellent work. Considering I had already set aside two bucketfuls of water, she had done me a solid. I awarded her with a beautiful water bottle. She was all over the place about how she was my favorite.

A decade back, when I was living at Ardente's, I had a strong liking for his step-sister, Super. She was an avid learner of almost anything that caught her eye. For me, anyone who possessed that trait was destined to be my friend for life. We used to take the graveyard shift every day up until almost dawn. I had missed most of my freshman and sophomore high school years because of school fees. Most of my colleagues would jump in joy whenever a teacher came in to send them away to clear their balances. I, on the other hand, would scream in pain from the inside. For a guy in boarding school, the school jester had nicknamed me 'the day scholar'. It was a good thing social media was not all that popular way back then, I would have been the center of attention for trending memes and hashtags.

Super had taught me one simple thing, I wasn't in control of my past, but my future? I was *sur contrôle*. After leaving her place, a decade later, we had had zero communication. Just like Ardente, she had new baggage—*Sourire*. While in college, a crafty man had managed to convince her that having sex often was excellent soul food. She had fallen for the trick, *viande contre la viande*, a lie that men often told their women. Several years later, she was the proud mother of a less bouncy baby boy—*he was standing on his two feet for all sake*. I was less lucky, her next visit was not likely to happen sooner or later. She had earned some recognition though. The people around called her the doctor. As a trained nurse, at the diploma level, I thought that was way overboard.

The day was less fun after I felt my respect had been tarnished. A few moments later, I headed out for the main house. In the study was Nuit. After tending to the guests, her final resort was reading. I liked her zeal, much like mine was back then. Her instincts greatly assumed I was a lover of fiction. So, she handed to me a copy of *La Mutilation,* a novella whose blurb talked of a young girl's success after escaping circumcision. I held it on my hand for a while before I tucked it into my back pockets. I was in no mood for reading. I took a great interest in her study but felt a little less obliged to help. Before I knew it, I had dozed off on a couch next to her. A lot was in my mind and I had no idea why I had voluntarily agreed to self-shame.

In my short siesta, my mind was all over my past. It seemed like it haunted me while I was in my composure. After Félicité had moved next to our house, and my brother not being around for a while, I had no other option but to reconsider my options. At first, it was simple innocence as I stared at her walking past out compound. She acted as if she didn't notice I was there. That did a number on me. After what seemed like a case of swallowing one's pride, I decided to follow her and ask the lady out. I was sure our encounter would end negatively, but I held on to that glimmer of hope inside me in a hope to rekindle my old flame.

"So, the dumb have finally spoken … "

Those were her very first words when I approached her.

"I hope you ain't referring to the dumb, as in the stupid kind. Because I'm not that."

She looked at me and then smiled. The rational part of my being was all for not falling for her tricks, albeit my reasonableness being strong, I fell for her once again. She was at that moment going to church. I was not a great fan of religion; but since impressing her was my mission, I did whatever it took. The trend continued for about three weeks. After that period, I could swear I had no grudge with her before. It was me and her against the world. No one around could stop us.

It reached a point, while we were in our daily walks, where I decided to hold her hands and re-propose. She was less enthusiastic about it. Like before, she gave me a blank look and then ignored me. I kept asking myself what I was lacking. If she had been convinced by my brother, of all people, then I at least owed myself a chance. He was less smart. I was the brains in the family. Despite being of average height, and having a super skinny frame, I didn't think that was the reason. That was the genesis of my many rejections from women. It sounded pretty ironic at that time, I had fine hair, a beautiful face—*yeah, for a man, and on top of it all, I was a smart guy*. I guessed that didn't count in her potential-boyfriend-to-be-handbook.

It took me about three years before I ever came back there. My homecoming was a bit different. I was on campus and I had a good track record for never having had sex with any girl in my neighborhood—*that was what every responsible parent would have been proud of.* I had thought of Félicité as being the one. For many years, I had convinced myself I loved her. Maybe that was one-sided. Like a one way street, I was walking by myself. At that time she was not around her home. Word went around that she was continuing her high school studies upcountry. The place seemed very lonely without her. I was with my brother, Ami, at that time.

Then Cécile happened. After having one too many doses of boredom, my mind was sent into temporary bipolar states. It was a good thing that my mood swings never resorted to violence. I simply kept to myself and solely concentrated on reading literature. My favorite picks were research papers on physics, computer science, and philosophy. My mind was full of ideas, and for moments, I felt immersed into endless realities of fantasy.

I had noticed a beautiful lady passing by our gate, across the road, for the past few days. She looked way above my league. I thought approaching her would break my already fragile heart again. I had no other alternative but to listen to my heart. However, my desires and sexual-drive hormones had something else to say.

One fine evening, on a Friday, at around three o'clock, Ami challenged me to say hi to her. She was coming straight from her farm. It was about ten minutes away from my place. My place was located downhill, so it felt nice to see her walk down. She was with her sister. At that point I cared much less about sibling connections, my mind was fixated on her. She was about 5'6" tall, had hazel eyes and super brown skin, and was moderate in terms of her body size. I had pumped in a few pounds after I started hitting out the gym, that made our bodies very compatible. Nobody around would say I was dating a girl older than me— *believe me, my face sold me out.*

From our talk, I got to learn her full name, and what she disliked. It turned out that I had met up with her on several occasions, while she was still a young girl. When it came to the part where I confessed I had earlier been afraid of approaching her, she laughed herself off. She said she thought I was smarter than that. I liked the fact that during that time, I wished she had been in my life from before. Our conversations were open, fun, and exciting.

Every day I would help her out on her farm. I hated tilling the ground, but it felt fun and painless. For moments I felt like I was her protector and her world. For a fortnight, I didn't notice my brother had been following me to my adventures, Cécile's sister was also there, but we never had any idea we were with them.

What thrilled me the most was that after work every day, we would stop just about five minutes next to her home. We would grab colas, and chips, and then hold each other's hands and lean against each other just for the pleasure of it. The road was less busy and the chances of anyone passing by were one in nothing. On the first day, I held back, but on day two I was all over her, and we had our first kiss. It was magical and I felt like the whole universe had opened up to us. The milky way galaxy was spinning, while nebulae, light years away, were glowing and shining their brilliant cloudy colors.

The last week was my beautiful girlfriend's birthday. I gave her a cardigan as a gift. Most of my peers had told me to have sex with her at that time. That didn't feel right to me. I had known her for a very short period and trivial matters like sex had to wait. I hadn't even had any STI tests with her. I was curious though, but I asked her. She said she would never be okay with it, not in a million years. I had to meet her parents first, and then officially announce my new relationship status to my parents. I thought of that as overkill and hence decided to go back to college. At least, academic disciplines had fewer demands.

It was *félicitations* for me, I had managed to blow up my chances of ever having sex in my home turf, all because of being a gentleman. That was when I swore solemnly not to ever date a girl from my neighborhood.

After waking from my long nap, Nuit and her sisters were nowhere to be seen. The kitchen door that led to the study was locked and I had to open it just to get to the outside. It was already dusk, and the chickens were already getting to their nests. There were chirps from birds getting ready for the night, I did bet they were in for dating. I surprisingly met Réveiller at the outside kitchen boiling water at a huge pot. When she saw me, she felt a spark of joy fill within her. I was a bit curious about her sudden change of heart. She notified me of her eagerness to see me head to the 'showers'. I laughed at her final statement very loudly. If she only knew what the word meant. Truly, her lack of grasp for the semantics was way overboard.

I quickly took a 'shower' as she had stated earlier. The water in the bucket I was using was very hot. I had to get creative; I took my panties and used them as a makeshift *douche*. I noticed my torn socks and quickly took them. Maman was right outside the bathroom. She looked like she was in a great hurry, so I went hurriedly to 'my room' and changed. I wore a look that said '*less classy but could impress a whole lot of people*' and left for Nuée's place.

It was like he had noticed me coming. That saved me the effort of going over to his place. We walked for about five minutes before he called a motorcycle to pick us up. I hated that form of transport, but I had to give in. We were headed for Ne Pas, a small urban center. There was not much to it. Just some rusty old buildings, excuses for shops, and a church. After setting foot 'ashore' we walked in the dark for a few minutes, while he made some calls, and finally reached a stop at a *carrefour*.

From the opposite direction, I could spot a girl coming our way. She was about my height but way skinnier. Even in the dark, her ebony black skin wasn't noticeable. To make it worse, her dark

outfit made her look like the *Fantôme de Ne Pas*. She was all
excited to see me. As always, whenever I would meet up with
girls, I was ready for a hug. My hands were wide open, but she
extended hers for a handshake. She then hugged her boyfriend
for forever as she giggled. They moved aside and talked about
their talk. It took them about five minutes to straighten out their
'family drama' but it felt like millennia were passing for me. It
was like I had discovered the solution to time travel. I traveled
faster than light, and then came back in time for torment from
their *tête à tête*.

They parted ways and Nuée was all over telling me about how he
loved his girlfriend, about how they were having sex *vingt quatre
sur vingt quatre* without any break. I felt like it was none of my
business knowing how many times they were making love. I
tolerated his perversion until we reached his place. On our way,
we met with four guys, around his age, with a girl. Without saying
a word, he quickly grabbed her arm and then held on to her waist
as they walked. They all looked fine from the look of things,
including her, I had sensed a false alarm. My mind had already
prepared me for an encounter with them. According to my brief
calculations, taking them down would be a piece of cake.

At Nuée's place, we found his mother serving dinner. It was a
mountain of *xima* and kale. The latter was a stew, composed of
that single ingredient and salt. After the usual pleasantries, of
how I had been gone away for a while and my prospects for the
future, we dived in. I only ate a few handfuls before I decided I
had to leave. I headed out slowly. Sourire was sleeping peacefully,
however, his nice comfort ended all of a sudden. He started
crying, his grandma took him from his colt and stood him next to
her. Out of necessity, he suddenly started peeing on the floor. I
looked in awe as the droplets of pee danced from the ground to

the food laid down there. No one around seemed to care. The lady got a hold of his male member and then told him that was how men were supposed to help themselves, by holding it. It seemed obvious that the kid had no idea what her saying meant, all he did was look at her. A plate was set ready for him, as I left, I saw the kid gobbling up the food with pride. I Stopped for a second to look at him and then left.

After what had happened the day before, I knew getting full would only make things difficult for me, Jacqueline would make sure I had eaten. The night was dark, and the moonlight, well … it was not far-reaching. I walked stealthily to the 'main' kitchen. Everyone was all quiet, and then, out of nowhere, I heard voices of chatter. Inside the kitchen, I saw two unfamiliar faces, a guy and a lady. They were all ebony black. I liked their skin tone, I had a fetish for girls with either ridiculously pale or dark skin. They brightened their smiles when they saw me. After a few introductions; the guy said his name was Michaël. He was proud to tell me that the lucky lady, Joanne, beside him was his sister. I nodded my head in humor. He had failed in matching up his semantics. I took a brief look at the lady. She was about 5'10" tall, while her sibling was about an inch shorter, her slouching shoulders made them appear to have the same height. Her hair was short and well combed. I didn't know if it was lust at first sight, but I had fallen for her *à l'instant*. She had large bright eyes and a slender frame. I could judge from the way she was sitting, that she had huge posteriors too. After noticing I was keen on staring at her, she smiled back at me. I looked down and then blushed. She had gotten me.

On my rookie day at that place, Béatrice had offered to let me take her seat at the kitchen. It was like her throne, one she was not willing to give up easily. After a day or two, she started calling dibs on the chair. I had no other option but to let go. It was a good thing there were spare plastic seats in her new house. When I met her for the first time, I had pictured her as a very mean old lady, people around had given me tales of her waywardness, it was after knowing her that I realized those were ill placed assumptions. I took a seat next to Nuit. At the room's entrance was the old lady to the left. Next to her was Jacqueline, cooking *le repas*. At the far right were the strangers. I sat at the center with Réveiller and Maman next to me. Food was being served. The chef was putting final touches to her meal. It was like I had timed the food serving.

Michaël held in his hand a device with a screen. It looked like a mobile tablet, however, upon closer inspection I realized it was a mobile DVD player. It looked sleek. The owner was around Nuit's age, and my best guess was he was trying to impress her. That guy reminded me of how men would do anything to get the attention of the girls they liked, I too was a victim, and soon enough, his sister would be reaping those benefits. He said it had run out of battery power. All that time I was looking at Joanne's outfit. She wore a baseball jacket, tight pants, and a purple t-shirt. We had never talked before, but our body language was getting us by just fine.

Our plates were garnished with sardines, kale, and *xima*. It was the same diet all over again. There was no end to their repeated dietary cycles. I could swear I hated them for putting me to that torture. If only they tried something different. I grabbed a plastic cup of water. I observed like before, patriarchy at play; the males had their hands first washed, and then the ladies followed. To make it worse, the same water that I used was what everyone else used. Mother tradition was truly an unhygienic lady.

After finishing our meals everyone, excluding me, engaged themselves in a discussion led by Béatrice. After becoming fully proficient in Dholuo, she had started her notoriety for using the language whenever she saw fit. I expected them to consider my presence and at least use Swahili, but none of them had thought about it. With no one else to talk to, I held on to my phone dearly and then started reading through ebooks. It was their occasional bursts into Swahili that gave me the context of what they were saying. It seemed like they were arguing whether Maman would make a good wife for Michaël. That sounded a bit gross; considering the guy was almost twice her age. Maman was upset with them.

Their debate got heated and that forced the latter to lash out at them. She was met with hostility from Béatrice, who threatened to whup her. I tried to go for her defense, but my visitor status prompted me not to. I just sat in the sidelines, hoping the madness would come to an end. At last, Jacqueline announced that it was sleep time. She had to prepare for work, and there was a long day ahead for everyone the following morning. We walked our 'guests' outside and parted ways with them. I longingly looked at Joanne as she left the compound, her silhouette disappearing in the dark, what remained was a figure of a being growing darker and darker.

As we headed out to our room, I didn't say a word to anyone, I was too exhausted to. Nuit led the way with her lamp. I lay in bed with a thud. I cared less for the duvet beside me; I simply wore my pajamas and slept like hell was never on earth. I heard faint sounds of the girls talking, and they faded away from the way I slept. That was it, I could hear them no more.

The following morning, I had woken up early. I wasn't served with the daily doses of repeated proof for existential existence. I had at least gotten up in time to delay it for eternity. It was cold outside and everyone was either asleep or planning to get up. It was cold outside. I could feel the chill inch its way down my back. The sight around was spectacular, it was like the excessive blue light; which manifested and brightened the terrain, had been replaced by a magnificent reddish filter, *excellent eclairage nocturne*. I looked at the beautiful view in delight.

Since sleep was not coming to me at any time soon, I took the initiative to combat my infant stage of insomnia. I sat on a stool, which lay outside, and then began thinking about the universe. That thought lasted until I couldn't reconcile the concepts of Newtonian classical physics and the more complex quantum mechanics of modern physics. It was odd that during that time, a holiday of all times, I was overheating my mental system with overly complex and trivial theorems—*which would break down a quantum computer*. As a self-proclaimed nerd, I was knowledgeable in more fields than I could imagine. The only problem was that with the fast-rising number of educational bodies, I had no certification to back my claims.

Like a petrified student at the school of Hogwarts, I sat on that chair without realizing time was passing. For a second I thought Einstein's special theory of relativity was coming to play; I had managed to travel faster than the speed of light, and then something great happened, I was able to leap across the space-time curve and slow down my time, I had essentially traveled in time, and then I was back, at least several hours later. The guys around had postponed breakfast upon Jacques's request. He, however, delayed their long-awaited meal and arrived at around eleven. That was when I was coming to my senses. It seemed like the people had managed to get a grasp of my character, whenever I was in deep thoughts, derangement was the last thing I ever wanted.

As usual, Jacques announced his arrival with blaring music. Like someone people had never seen in forever, everyone gathered around his car to welcome him. I thought that was a bit primitive, even for those guys, but well …. the heart wanted what it wanted. He alighted with Étienne, his wife, and daughter. The ladies had over-dressed, but they looked fine all in all. The latter went to the house, while the former stayed outside with me. A table was set for us and breakfast started coming in. We were served with mashed potatoes, fried eggs, (it was a good thing they were not scrambled. In as much as I liked *Les américains, omelette espagnol* was my personal best), *thé avec du lait*, and boiled bananas. The last was a deal-breaker because they lacked salt and oil, just boiled without even being peeled off.

I took my breakfast with zeal, but my perfect harmony was being trampled over by Jacques. He kept pestering me to 'eat', 'eat', until I got a little unhappy. He was one of the few people in the world who you would never seem to get annoyed at. I looked at him with a look that said, 'not assuring'. I later noticed his pestering dwindling, it seemed he had gotten the message.

After the hearty brunch, Jacques announced that we would be taking a walk around. In his words, it was not great for me to leave without ever seeing his former school. Our trip was joined in with two other guys, Avion and Blanc, who came in the course of the meal. We were all set for an epic road walk. I felt especially skeptic of it because it would only last for a brief while. I thought his wife would join us; but it was then that I realized, she had not even bothered to greet us. I assumed she was either having domestic or work problems. I cared less about it.

Throughout the whole journey, Blanc was our designated guide.
His super white t-shirt seemed to affirm his name very well. He,
Avion and Jacques were immersed in endless chatter. I, on the
other hand, tried to listen to the beat of the music. My earphones
were, however, becoming ineffective at a quicker rate. The
disturbance from motorcycles passing by was unbearable. We
passed by the famous swampy grassland, Macérage, it was where
my dad and almost every male member of my extended family
used to herd. Its sheer size was amazing. There was a huge water
pan at its center. Whenever the sun was at it earnest, hitting the
foreheads of the herders with zeal, the cattle would rush to the
pan and quench their thirsts. There was however a menace of
water reeds, which grew all over the place and were threatening
the survival of the pan.

I felt a little inspired by the view. I promised myself I would write
a poem about it. I felt my feet crush through the small pebbles
and the finely eroded footpath, it was probably communally
made. Avion had switched back and forth between Dholuo,
Swahili, and Maragoli. For a moment, I was confused, the whole
step of the way. The linguistic context switches were good, they
enabled me to get a hold of what they were saying. As we walked
I noticed the spectacular madness of the local administration. In
the course of their road-making, they had left very huge holes,
after their efforts of digging sedimentary rock, for paving their
roads. During the rainy season, I was told that the holes and the
roads would fill up with water, and anyone not careful enough
would meet their untimely death.

The previous year, a family in a very posh car had met their
demise in one of those holes. They were driving at a time when

cats and dogs, in excess, were falling from the skies. Instead of taking a detour and using the road from Ne Pas, and around Jacques's home; they decided to take a shortcut, after all, they had a luxury car. It was a very big Renault SUV, midnight black, with state of the art designs, which proved too good for their last-minute rush. In the car was a lady, a wife to the owner of a house we were just passing. It was to my direct left, amid all the under-suburbanization, on my side was a row of super-sophisticated houses.

It was like walking in a suburb, in downtown Naïrobi. At the center was a very huge bungalow. The owner was said to have had no meaningful education in his early life. No one could say they knew what he did for a living, but surprisingly, he lived the life of an upper-middle-class person. At the comforts of their homes, people silently gossiped of his wayward ways. Word went around like wildfire about how he had joined a 'devil-worshiping-cult', and all his wealth not being legit.

The wife was in a rush to see her husband, the devil worshiper, and little did she know that things would go sideways. Just next to her house, the road had flooded to about a foot high. The holes had also filled to the brim. In an effort to cut a corner, she saw herself and her children (*all three*) falling into the hole. They had their safety belts on and the windows were tightly shut. The hole was about fifteen feet deep. There were cries from neighbors around as the tragedy was setting its course. The husband went to the scene immediately and warned all the divers that were ready to save the then fragile lives, not to do so. Amidst their outcry, he used his force and influence to caution them. After what seemed like a daunting moment, the people around witnessed deaths they could have prevented. It was then that the long-held theory, of him being in a cult, was established and affirmed.

As we walked by, a year down the line, the holes had not been filled, and there was no sign of any future change. I was slightly frightened by wealth and everything else that came along with it. We walked for another ten minutes across farmlands and finally reached a road. Motorcycles were still reckless. They drove at full speed, and if anyone wasn't careful, they would meet their end. Jacques was excited to point us to the direction of his former school, Ne Pas. The trading center around it also went by the same name. We didn't get the opportunity to get inside, but the view from the fences was just as fulfilling.

Blanc decided to leave us off after we had passed the school gate. He announced his home was up in the hills; a call of invitation from him was met by very polite rejections, in as much as we wanted to visit every nook and cranny, getting worn out in the process was the last thing we wanted. We made a last tour around the school fences and then headed for home. I put on my headphones and listened to my music playlist. I wasn't an avid talker at that moment. It was great that Étienne and Avion were busy keeping Jacques company. Before I knew it, we were back to the Macérage.

The sun was overhead and my feet were hurting from the long walk. Jacques was quick to give us fun facts. It was the former president, Mwai Kibaki, who had commissioned for the building of the water pan. Fast forwarded a decade later, it was in a state worse than intended. I was fascinated by a gang of five boys, who were butt naked, and skinny dipping with jerrycans—*as nonconventional lifebuoys*. There were also several women taking baths in the nearby bushes. My inner perverted-self was pressuring me to go see, but my inner sense was in total control.

The long walk landed us to Avion's place. Jacques forced us to make a stopover there. It was like sailing in a pirate ship and then stopping by somewhere just to replenish supplies. He took a cup of cold pot-water and then directed us to rest under the shade of a mango tree. After what seemed like a never-ending moment of listening to his chatter, we finally left. They had all been about how Jacques would host Avion in case he would ever find himself in Naïrobi. I knew that was only blatant small-talk. It was a good thing that back, at his place, I was awaited by a table full of unsophisticated food. I was, however, grateful, for the last thing I wanted to do was have the hands feeding me bitten—*no would ever like fork.*

The meal was a hearty one. It was the usual sardines, *xima*, and 'traditional' vegetables. I took no notice until I was full. I took a cup of water to wash everything down. Réveiller and Nuit came to clear the table. I saw Étienne catching glimpses of them as they came by, they, however, took little notice of him. As their uncle, I had some protective instinct for them, that was why I was alarmed with Étienne's excitement over them.

Later that evening, after not bothering to follow Jacques and his horde of friends to town, I headed out to Ardente's place. After borrowing his mother's boots the other day, I had feared she would have been raging mad. That morning when I was returning them, I met her at her door. She was very composed and less alarmed when I returned her *outils*. She had greeted me and invited me in. I was served with a jug of tea and fried bananas. I couldn't swear I was having a great time, but that was awesome! Since I had been in a hurry, for nothing really, I had left her without a chat and promised her a visit later in the evening.

I found her at her homestead, around the center were two trees where we sat. She was all smiles when she was greeting me. I felt excited about having to converse with her. A decade earlier, while crashing at her place, she had labeled me a thief. She assumed I had stolen two hundred shillings from under her bed. I was in my defense, but she was all for her juvenile delinquent son. I was a little hurt back then, but it seemed time had healed my scars. I had long since forgotten about her favoritism. I was looking around every corner for her daughter, Lucie. We had been very good friends way back. She had assured me that her daughter was away for work, working as a gold miner's assistant. It would have made a lot of sense to call her a gold digger.

My talk with Ardente's mom, I never got her name, revolved around my childhood past and about my dad. She narrated to me how I had gotten there as an infant. My late grandmother by then had my father as her favorite son. By default, I followed in his footsteps. I got a lot of preferential treatment and it hurt the former when I left and never came back. The narrator was a little sad that my dad had decided to leave his birthplace for good, and head out to a place where his family was far off. She tried to reason with me about the benefits of living next to family.

I felt moved by her speech and made a resolve to buy land around that place and settle down hopefully. The land that grandfather had left was very small, and I thought that was partly the reason dad didn't want any part of it. The other reason was witchcraft. Some part of him still believed that people around that place would bewitch any successful members of his family.

Even in his long-distance, most of his older kids had turned out far worse than those left behind. We all laughed at my conclusion.

After talking for a while, I felt the motherly connection between her and me growing. I had a psychological problem. My mother had abandoned me at the tender age of three. I was left under the care of my father. From those early years on, I was taken round countless homes, of his 'wives', until I had no real definition of who a real mother was. By the time I was ten, I was sent to our Nakūru farm. There it was like I was on my own. Living with my brothers was like hell, and that was the beginning of my psychological dysfunctions.

Fantasies of her caring for me as my mother flared through my head. I felt happy that she was there for me as a kid. How she went to school with me. All those school events that no one ever bothered to attend, she was there. Her final words made me zap from my momentary thoughts. She was about to head out somewhere before it was dark. She politely asked for a favor from me, and it was hard to decline. Her eldest child, Foi, whom she kept referring as my 'sister', had a child. She wanted me to take the kid's certificate of birth, to her home in Naïrobi. I was to liaise with her and give her the document. As a parting gift, she gave me Foi's contact details and headed for her house.

I waited briefly. The sight around was magnificent, the sun was setting, and the orange skies filled the surrounding with a feel similar to the twilight. She later came out with a brown envelope. I saw the look in her eyes, one that was happy and full of pride. I got hold of it and later assured her it would be delivered safely. As the dark slowly enveloped the place, I received newer insight; the place my father had denied me knowledge of, was turning out to not be bad after all. I walked with pride and zeal as I left her compound. For the first time, Les Derniers en Appelant was silent. I wondered if all the nutcases in the area had finally gotten well, or maybe they were running out of business. I thought that would be one of the nicest things happening for a change.

Fast-forwarded to the next day, everything went on as usual until around ten o'clock, when Jacques arrived. It amazed me how the folks there would readily starve themselves in the morning. They would deliberately take their breakfast at around eleven in the morning. Things would change when Jacques was around, they would push back their clocks by an hour or so. His music was louder than ever. He played the francophone African version of kompa music, or something similar to Afro-fusion. I was very less interested in the announcement of his arrival. For starters, he had promised to take me to the Tanzanien border, and the western frontier of Moustique. Days had passed, and not seeing a fulfillment of his promise made me uneasy. The prospect of journeying there was dim. I simply sat transfixed to my chair. A simple 'hi' from him lighted down my spirits, and I remained in my sorry state for a while.

I had a disastrous breakfast of 'black tea', and 'plain rice' I believed I never sent them a memo stating I was lactose intolerant—well... the food they served spoke volumes. Jacques announced that we would be going to the Tanzanien border for a walk. I had to kill time until one o'clock when we left. I carried my laptop. It had been several days since I shut it down, for power saving reasons. I felt that juicing it up would be the right thing to do. In the village, driving with Jacques was like a live motion enactment of the a-from-nothing-to-everything parade. Jacques had lowered down all the car windows. He intended to catch a glimpse of everyone in their homesteads. He would call out their names and greet them. I thought it as being weird, but he enjoyed it the whole step of the way. We drove downhill for around five minutes. The road was rocky, but the lush green vegetation and the winding of it made it superb. As we approached the town, the settlements looked fancier, and just next to Ardente's dad's rental houses, we made a turn to Jacques's townhouse.

A few yards from Jacques's house was my lady cousin's house. It was a state of the art house. In layman's terms, a bungalow with a basement and upstairs rooms. Plus, it had an attic. It had an awful burnt-sienna coloring, which I hated. The thing that gave it glamour was the design choice of having opaque glass for all its windows. I wondered why my blood relative was living large, and I, on the other hand, was a mere pauper. I was on the verge of being homeless and had no prospect of ever getting employed.

Jacques lived in a gated community. There was the main gate, which connected countless neighborhoods, and another one, a few yards away, which led to his house. His section had five houses in it. His wife was living quite the life, I thought. Judging from their sheer size, the houses had at least five rooms. They all had outdoor porches, which connected to the main doors. They were like small lobbies, where one could rest or have a cup of coffee. The lawn was olive green, and the bushes were well-trimmed. At the far edge was a water well. To my surprise, there were no outdoor toilets. That was a big blow to me because I hated using toilets with seats—*the splashing water gave me hemorrhoids and a tingly feeling down there.*

Inside the house, Jacques was welcomed by two of his housemaids. One of them was a strikingly beautiful lady in her late teens—*her smile was spectacular by the way,* the other was a middle-aged woman, who I cared less about. They brought to the table a bottle of chilled cola and grapes. At the center of the room was a glass table, and around it were leather couches, with shiny round silvery metals studded on them. Opposite the direction of the door was a huge television set, about forty inches, and a multimedia sound system. A huge wall cabinet, filled with cutlery, housed the electronics. Étienne was busy connecting his phone to the devices wirelessly. His enthusiasm was undoubtedly far reaching. I could tell he was making himself comfortable.

From the hallway, connecting the living room and the other rooms, Heureux came in. She quickly grabbed the TV remote and tuned in a kid animation program similar to *Dora L'explorateur.* I found a way to tease her. Whenever I said, *«Je m'appèle Heureux»* she would respond angrily by saying, *«Non, tu es Heureux pas. Je suis Heureux, je suis Heureux, … »* That made me laugh. Funny though, my little teasing helped me create a rapport with her. Within no time, I was playing and laughing with her. It felt good since, up there in the village, she had totally ignored me.

After taking my final sips of the cola, I placed my empty glass on the table. Apparently, my kiddish antics made me finish last. Like in a restaurant, the maids came in and cleared the table. They later came in with a bowl of steamed fish, scrambled eggs mixed with kale, *xima*, and ice-cold water. It was a self-service buffet, so

I served myself huge chunks of fish. For once, I did enjoy my lunch. It was a nice break from my usual cliché of sardines. I took napkins set at the table and then cleaned my soupy hands.

 I remembered my laptop needed juice. The marvel of the house had made me forget it at the back of the car. After taking it, I naïvely asked Étienne where I could charge it. His response was that I should ask Belle-Mari, the older maid. My first steps outside the living room were a bit like Neil Armstrong's treadings on the lunar rocky paths. The hallway was big, it connected several rooms. I saw Belle-Mari sitting on a stool next to the kitchen. She had a huge piece of chicken breast, while her counterpart had a huge chunk of cake. Immediately they saw me, they hid their snacks inside their skirts. I felt disgusted and at the same time sorry for them. I tried hard to let them know that I was in no way concerned about their food thieving conquests.

«*Salut, je voudrais charger mon ordinateur, m'aider s'il te plaît.*»

«*Aller au salon … *»

«*Merci … *»

I began by greeting Belle-Mari and after asking her where I could charge, her response was for me to go back to the living room. Back there, the power extension cords were far off from where I could sit. If I were to wait till my machine had a full charge, that would have been understandable, however with a kid roaming in the house, I couldn't take any chances. After seeing my plight, Étienne asked me to follow him to his room. Heureux followed us while jumping up and down. She was very happy for having had made newer friends.

As I connected the device, I remembered Jacques's words to me after we had taken our lunch. He had said that if I were to use the toilets in the house, then all hell would break loose. The house would stink far worse than a skunk. His tone was serious, which meant he was meaning everything he was saying. The room had a bed with two bunkers. Étienne took the upper one, while the younger maid took the bottom one. He said he was too afraid to even talk to her as they slept at night. In my mind, I pictured what would have happened if I were there. It was no wonder Jacques had left me back in the village. Also, any sane man who failed to make a pass at a beautiful lady was either gay or something else according to my macho-man book. I started to get wary of myself, lest he made a pass at me.

Heureux kept pressuring me to take a nap with her. Her parents had instilled in her a daily routine of sleeping after lunch. Having new found friends, she felt it was her duty to share her precious moments with all her besties. She held on to both my arms and those of Étienne. He strongly resisted, which left me with the burden. The only thing that saved me was Jacques's announcement of us leaving at that instant. I slowly slipped my hands from hers and then ran. Across the hallway the two ladies sat while sipping glasses of cold water, they were living the life— la vie facile.

We took a turn to a dusty road. Like ants in a colony, motorcycles were passing us by without ending. The drive lasted for about five minutes. Jacques had talked of his brother having a rental house project in town. I was full of anticipation to see how it looked like. It seemed all my dreams were coming true. Unlike where Jacques lived, there was less business activity the more we approached his place. We took a turn left and then stopped at a newly finished construction site. I refused to leave the car. All I could see near the gate was a huge septic tank and an unmowed lawn. There were two houses, which Jacques estimated would cost about 5,000 shillings per month. Coupled with inflation and the rising costs of living; Étienne argued that the rent would keep going up. I smiled silently, knowing he had been at least smart for a change.

We didn't stay that long. I was glad our stop there wasn't much of a delay. I would have opted to bail on them. Since the path was a single lane, we had to reverse our way out to the main road. From there we drove to the main highway. There was no sign of the motorcycles ending. Huge trucks from neighboring Tanzanie lined up the road like ducklings in pursuit of their mother. I remembered telling Étienne to carry his identification right when we were leaving the house. He had refused adamantly. When I brought up the issue, Jacques made the most fun of him. That made him angry.

As we headed to the border, we saw more and more Tanzanien cars. There was more of personal cars than trucks. We started a small debate on the state of affairs in the East African region. Ouganda and Kenya were like the two brothers who loved each other. They were born from the same mom and she and daddy loved them dearly. They grew up to become fine young people. Everyone loved them and they prospered greatly amid their skeletons still haunting them. Unfortunately, daddy got another wife—*she had been previously married to daddy's cousin*. She came in with another kid, Tanzanie. Daddy didn't love him that much, and the original brothers had little enthusiasm for him.

With time, the latter managed to invade his brother's lands and successfully refused to honor a pact which united them. After things had gotten better and all loose ends had been tied, Tanzanie still didn't get it. He was rivaling his siblings in almost everything. The only places he managed to excel in were the arts—*that was good for him*. It was easy for him to enter his brothers' territory, roam freely, and conduct trade. However, the stringent rules he placed on his family made them dread visiting his home.

After receiving several calls on the road, Jacques made a stop in the middle of nowhere. We left the car to enjoy the cool breeze and stretch our feet. I was resistant at first but gave in when Jacques insisted. I took pictures of that godforsaken place we were in. I tried hard not to get closer to the bush—*for lack of a better term, I had serpent-phobia, I hated snakes.* And then, out of nowhere, a guy came to where we were. He was about 5'10" with a super skinny frame and a dark complexion. His safari boots created the impression that he was taller. His arrival was like that of Big Foot from a blockbuster film. He had very large feet, like a kitten in boots. One could imagine his shoes were wearing him. I laughed at the sound of that thought.

Jacques introduced him as his former school mate before we entered the car. I had taken my fill of photos and got in without question. I had memorized the words he always said whenever one took his car seat, *«Fixez vos ceintures de sécurité»*, he didn't forget at that time. His priority was always everyone's safety and avoiding the five-dollar penalty for not putting on the safety belt. He turned up the music volume to an extreme level, I hated his choice of music. I persevered with the hope of finally reaching Bord in time.

Bord was a single lane town, with its road turning hilly towards the border. We made a stop next to a police station, perhaps Jacques thought no one would bother messing his car near the police. The way we left the car suggested we were tourists. It was a good thing the people around there were used to the latter. Jacques's guy led the pack, I, however, followed along behind. I tried to keep up with Étienne's small-talk. He was a prick but sometimes he did teach me a thing or two. For instance, he was the one who showed me that plugging in my headphones' jack-pin deeply into my phone's audio jack would keep it firm and … He also showed me a neat trick on how to download movies online. In as much as I loved free things, I had solemnly vowed never to disrespect my fellow artists. I was all for going to the movie theater and watch my eyes out on the silver screen.

The guy led us into a small settlement, just like Ami's in Naïrobi. After maneuvering across countless hallways, we headed straight to his house. Inside, were two ladies and an infant. From the doorsteps, I could see the finely mopped floors, they had no tiles on them but were super beautiful. I followed along and took off my shoes, after seeing the others doing so. Jacques asked for a cup of water after we were done with all the pleasantries. For the record, I had a 'thing' with kids, so when the baby started crawling towards me, I felt it was my time to have fun with it. I patted its head and then handed it to one of the ladies, whom I presumed to be the mom.

Our stay over there wasn't bound to be long-lived. Jacques and his guy started leaving, and that was enough for us to leave also. In the house, the guy was referred to as Professeur by his wife, it was a nice step for me, not knowing his name was killing me. He told us that journeying across the border wasn't that bad. The only problem was if someone got caught by the authorities. He told us of how a Kenyane had been jailed there for three years because of not having a passport and a visa. My fears of getting close to the border started developing.

We got into the car and drove for a few minutes next to the border. Jacques parked the car next to three food trucks. Just as we were walking next to the border gates, a skinny guy on a motorcycle, with three of his colleagues asked us if they could give us a ride at a fee. They spoke in an accent you could only find in the neighboring country. We politely declined and headed north. After the gates, was a strip of no man's land. I was informed that I could pitch a tent there and live my life—*it would be a haven of nontax compliance, or endless drug abuse if I were a junkie.*

Out there was a stretch of concrete pavements. We walked into the Kenyane customs office compound. I was told that was where I could get clearance just in case I wanted to stay overnight in Tanzanie. Right after our customs office, we got into the Tanzanien one. It was very rusty and in need of maintenance. Professeur added that the Kenyanes were keen on injecting billions into beautification programs, while their counterparts, well ... not so much.

The customs on the other side was quiet. I could only see people with trading goods and foodstuffs. It was like small scale trade flourished over there because zero tariffs were imposed on them. As we were leaving the customs, I saw a sign that read, *«Ne repose pas sur le jardin»*, next to a garden. Jacques laughed at the thought of it and said that if anyone was caught taking their long nap, they would face a jury of heartless executioners.

The atmosphere, land, and everything in Tanzanie was not all different from what I had experienced in my country before. The only spectacular thing was that the people around there spoke with a different Swahili accent and never did openly in their native tongues, I guessed the censorship from their founding fathers was worthwhile. I hated how their currency had zero value. Something I could buy for a thousand in my home turf cost around twenty score of that amount.

 The dream of crossing the border wasn't all fun and glory as I had expected. I took a soda from a ridiculously tall glass bottle and got to take a dump in one of their toilets, they had no seats—*I had to squat my way down*. We left only with two bags of rice, which were supposedly cheaper.

That night, it was all fun and joy at Jacques's home. Michaël and Joanne were already around. Nuit informed me they had earlier been afraid of me, that was why I hadn't seen much of them on my first days. Michaël had brought in his portable TV. They were busy watching in the study. I could hear Joanne from the gate as I was arriving. *«Je suis en train de regarder»*, was her expression as she glued her eyes on the film before her. Jacqueline was in the kitchen with her mother. I joined them and started talking a little politics. My major highlights were about crossing the border and farting myself out in the foreign lands. They all laughed at my joke and then quickly forgot I was talking to them once Michaël had entered the room.

He was more talkative at that time. After realizing my

comprehension for the Dholuo tongue was wanting, I quickly left them. I headed for the study in the 'main' house, where Nuit and the others were. I had never been a fan of Afro-films, the way their storylines were sicklily twisted and had predictable endings made me hate them even more. Countless hours of inspiration from Hollywood content had made me quite the critique. If anything failed to match higher expectations, I would simply not follow it.

The room was darkly lit and full of stench, the kids were crammed in a row of seats. From their innocently lit faces, I could see an attentive people—*the power of art in action*. I took pride in simply seeing them. They were watching a Nigerian adventure film, *Olamiri et le Crocodile*. The storyline was sleek, but the CGI, graphics, and imaging were way off the charts. I hated to admit it, but it did seem nice to watch. For moments, about an hour, I was transfixed to my seat and focused on the West African story. What I liked about my cinéma audience was their silence. None of them talked while we were watching. Just when we were reaching the climax, the TV powered off.

It made a squishy sound before its screen went black. I looked at it in anger and even called it a 'tin can', everyone else laughed at my comment. Michaël laughed and said he would recharge it the day after. After telling him my electricity woes, he invited me to juice up our devices. I hadn't noticed that Joanne had been staring at me all that while. I quickly finished up my talk with him and joined in with his sister. Nuit had turned on the lights, which made the room look a little lively. I could finally see Joanne in detail.

Just when I thought we would talk, Jacqueline shouted at the top of her lungs, inviting us to take supper. The 'other' kids around left for their homes, my favorite ones remained though. Jacqueline had prepared chapati and tea for a change. My usual culinary habits had never prompted me to ever take breakfast like foods like hers. She sat on a stool, with a *tissu enveloppant* wrapped around her waist. It had dark green and brown colors. I was mesmerized by its beauty and kept looking at it. It was a good thing she hadn't noticed anything. She kept telling me to eat, just like her brother—*she was a pain…*

Then all over sudden, she came up with a very crazy suggestion, which I liked. She looked Joanne in the eye and then told her her plan. She began her argument with a call for peace. Her idea was trade for trade. She said that instead of people complaining about Michaël taking Maman, I should be given Joanne. Her emphasis was for the latter to start working hard in school if she wanted to have a shot with me. I looked at her and then smiled. Maman, however, had varying opinions. I couldn't blame her anyway, she was just a kid. I had started understanding her moments; whenever she was upset, I would talk nicely to her, and she would cool down.

The next day, I headed straight to Michaël's rendezvous point. I carried with me my laptop and my phone. They were all out of juice. He was wearing a faded black T-shirt and black shorts. His wide smile was enough proof he was happy to usher me—*to the juice factory*. After meeting at his gate, just next to Nuée's home, he told me to wait for a while. It took him about fifteen minutes to come around. I felt a little angry with him. However, the very fact that he was helping me made me cool down.

We walked down a rocky footpath, the one I had walked on most nights. An old lady, with a little girl passed by us. They were carrying basketfuls of bananas. I liked her effort, and couldn't help but stop her, and buy her wares. She was very thankful. After handing me my change, she couldn't stop herself from having small-talk with me. She narrated how my father had been a naughty boy back in his heydays. In her own words, he was the tall guy, who every girl in the village admired. It was too bad for her since she was a generation older than him.

We continued down the path as we chatted about Moustique. I made false promises to Michaël, telling him how I would host him in my house, in case he would ever come over to Naïrobi. That was the same thing Jacques told people he met, the only difference was that he was honest. I gave him my contact details seemingly hoping Joanne would get hold of them. Before I knew it, we had reached our destination. On the way, Michaël had made at least five stops, talking to people I had no idea of.

The Dholuo people were famed for being overly extravagant, and lavish. We approached a mud-walled house. It had a metal door and windows. From the inside, the owner had begun working on plastering the walls with cement. I liked his sense of style. There were leather couches, an 81 inch TV, a home theater, a glass table, and well … chickens. Michaël talked to the owner for a few minutes, before we were let in.

It didn't take me long before I felt bored. I had been pressured by my hosts to play them, gospel music, and then showcase to them previews of all the movies I had. I made an excuse about having had an urgent call. It was a good thing Nuée had been pestering me with calls. I tried hard to tell him to join me in, but he was a little adamant. After finally leaving my 'hell hole', I found Nuée a close distance from that house. He was all about having a 'beef' with my hosts. I couldn't debate with him, so I left. On my way, Jacques passed in his car. From the look of things, he was very drunk. I wished he were in the city, I wasn't a sadist, but seeing him harassed by the police would have been my joy.

On the next day, seeing that I hadn't charged my phone at all, Michaël opted to take me to another charging place. A few yards away from where we were before, we went to one of his uncle's place. It was a finely fenced and gated residence. It had mowed lawns and outside toilets. On the outside, we met with a fairly young lady—*to our surprise, she was in her late teens.* She was short, light, and not so beautiful. She also chewed on sugar cane while listening to music from her iPod.

I quickly liked her attitude when she lashed out at Michaël when he suggested he should charge our devices at their place. She said, 'What if I disagree?' He was lost for words for seconds. I decided to help him out by saying, 'We could just go.' She led us in and offered us what we needed. For once, I felt like I was in a place which understood me. All felt like home. I was at a new place, juicing up my babies while stealing glances at a girl I had just met. She was too busy to notice her new secret admirer. Since we had gone there very early, I hoped they would offer us some tea— *despite my growing impatience.* It seemed if I were a doctor, then I would have gotten more patients.

Our small paradise was shattered when the other house members came. First, it was a toddler, and then two of her brothers. They were teenagers who were around fifteen years of age. They came in with a liter of milk, and five loaves of bread—*that made me reminisce about Jesus' tales of feeding the five thousand, from my childhood storytelling.* I was relieved that my pangs of hunger had suddenly come to an end. However, after an hour-long wait, I knew my ulcers would continue eating me.

The latter, just like their predecessor, were just as inconsiderate. The only thing that made me keep up with my unease was the young kid. He was all over Michaël. They played in a not so good way until I got their attention. The latter spanked his ass, carried him on top of his shoulder, and then played Eskimo kissing with him. I felt disquited sitting next to that unfolding madness. The teens were seated comfortably on two large couches. I had placed my laptop on a glass table at the center. The power extensions lay on a huge wall cabinet which hosted the TV. With that, my power cord stood in their way—*they had to literally skip it.*

There was a huge freezer that stood opposite to where I sat. For a people living in the remotest depths of *Le règlement rural Kenyan,* they sure lived the life. One of the boys switched the channel from a kid entertainment show to an Indian blockbuster. I was very interested. I liked the sheer lies they told us. From how a guy would punch a wall and break it, to how another would fight a thousand men. Those were lies worth watching.

The girl would occasionally come to where we were to see her phone, which was charging. She wore very tight shorts, and a dark fitting T-shirt, which complimented her complexion. As she walked, I got carried away by her rhythmical movements from her rear. It was as if she was aiming to arouse my desires. Michaël had asked me to transfer Nigerian films from a DVD to his flash storage. Whenever the lady passed, I would suspend whatever I was doing just to see her. The former felt furious, but I couldn't help it. By the time she dressed up and left, I felt as if something

I had was gone for good.

I was grateful for once that Michaël had been considerate of my tastes. We walked slowly to my place after I was through. I expressed my interest in our lady host, his cousin, but he warned me she was bad news. From the looks of it, she had countless lovers and zero brains. I held my head down as we walked past his homestead. Luckily for me, Joanne was at her place, combing her hair. She blew me a kiss after I had smiled at her. I felt my blood jumping out of my eyes, they were red with an unexplained victory.

That afternoon was a big one for me. Jacques was at his home making merry with his friends. His car was parked right next to a table around him, which was set full of liquor. One of his car doors was open, to ensure maximum sound came from his music box. Like a mad man, he stood up and then uttered gibberish, he then danced a few styles. It was unfortunate that he noticed me. Out of respect I went to where he was and said hi. He held his bottle of whiskey and then politely asked me to take a sip for the stomach. I liked religion, but whoever purported that had lied. I couldn't have any of his craziness, so I slowly left. I went to the kitchen to see if there was anything I could bite. To my luck, there was a bowl of sardines and xima. I was sure whatever was not killing me would sure make my life a living hell, but I had to take my chances.

As I swallowed each chunk, I shed a tear. I struggled to the last one, I was finally *hors du combat*. From the look of things, I knew I would get the boredom of my life that day. However, when I saw Jacques come to where I was, my perspective changed. He invited me on a short road trip to Colline Buffle, a center several miles away. I couldn't refuse the invitation. We were to leave in five. I quickly dressed and joined them. We had with us, Avion, and Étienne. They kept silent as the car sped along the road, leaving trails of dust behind—*the passers by cursed as we passed them, in retaliation, Jacques uttered, 'Take that for a snack! Ha-ha'*. We wandered around one of the remotest places I had never been to. It was enlightening but somehow less fun than I had expected.

All I could see were tiny houses and a reddish-brown road. The North American Space Agency was injecting billions into the Mars expeditions just to see the red planet. I believed it would have made more sense if they would simply come to where we were. The area was sparser than where we lived. There were vast grasslands and sugar plantations. I enjoyed the drive until we reached Colline Buffle. On our drive, we passed a strangely named center—*Le Coin Mortel* . It was a sharp corner, where you would crash accidentally into an oncoming car.

As usual, Jacques told us to get out of the car for fresh air. Avion walked with overrated pride. It was like he was trying to make a statement. Maybe the guys around needed to know he was finally rolling with a car. It was the least of my expectations to meet with my former college-mate, Safin. He was a living testimony of a 'from-nothing-to-something-pleasant-for-the-least' At first I didn't recognize him. From what I gathered, he was one of Jacques' students from his peer teaching days.

Back in college, I and Safin used to live a hard life. Most of the students with cash lived closer to school in super-expensive hostels. We, however, lived five miles from our lecture halls. That meant walking for about an hour and a half to school. Education was truly the key to getting our feet sore. It was a good thing the doors to our classes were always open. Our houses were simple single rooms with basically bed and table-chair setups.

We reminisced for a while about the good old days. Jacques, however, cut us short and directed us to a nearby bar. The center was very small. Just like Ne Pas, it had rows of shops. The only newer thing was a motorcycle shade. The people around were taller, and darker—*the true Negroes*. Inside the bar were two attendants. They wore black aprons, and had their caps branded, '*Le Bistro de Colline Buffle*'. I liked their sense of style. The music was abnormally loud. According to Avion, if I were to get high, then the sound would become a mere whisper. I laughed at the sound of that. I knew his bird-brain had no sense of reasonableness.

The bar's entrance had a counter in its direct left, with several rows of couches—like a tiny lobby. A few feet from it was another entrance to a huge lounge. In it were almost a hundred tables, with four seats each. For many, that was a haven for merrymaking. After securing a spot, Safin called on the attendants. Jacques ordered a bottle of brandy. Next to us was a middle-aged lady taking sips from her *Le chateau du Nord*, an expensive bottle of *rosé* wine. It was evident that the people around had very sophisticated tastes. I liked that.

As the others were making themselves at home with the brandy, I went to the toilets. As if things couldn't get any worse, a drunk

lady came next to me while I was taking a piss. She was all about
how men were animals. Out of courtesy, I ignored her. However,
she became too much of a nuisance, and kept blocking my way.
After asking her what she wanted, all she could say was, 'I need
your help, buy me a beer please.' I couldn't take any of that, so I
left her in her sorry state.

I found the guys halfway drunk. At first, I sat alone on a very tall
stool called *Je n'ai pas de souffrance* . It was a symbol of having
tranquility. I never knew drunk people were humorous. If I had
known before, then I wouldn't have wasted my little cash on
stand up comedy. The people were full of themselves. The most
remarkable sight was seeing a guy, in his early twenties, grinding
on a middle-aged woman. Lest the guys thought I was bailing on
them, I went to where they were. All I wanted was to sit with
them and sip a cola and then leave. However, their pestering on
me to drink got me somewhat infuriated. I stood from where I
was and then left, having lied that I was taking a phone call.

I trekked down to Ne Pas while looking from behind to see if
they were following me. The coast was clear. I ignored Jacques's
calls all the way. I made an effort to call Nuée. It was a good
thing we would meet at Ne Pas. I never knew walking was such a
pain. I walked until the muscle connecting my heel and calves
became sore. I could feel a sharp pain whenever I raised my leg. I
estimated I would take around an hour and a half to meet Nuée.

At the bar, I could swear my desires were getting the better of me
when I saw the lady grinding. She was around six feet tall and
very dark. She wore tight brown pants and a blue blouse. She
stood bent in front of the guy, and then slowly rotated her body
around his groin, relative to the rhythm of the music. My eyes
were locked on them until I couldn't take it anymore. I knew my

intellect couldn't allow me to do anything stupid, so I left.

I found Nuée at Ne Pas. He was with a girl and two guys, around his age. I immediately went to where they were. The girl left, and so did the others. I had a lot on my plate and so I couldn't care any less. Nuée was very judgmental when I narrated my ordeal. Instead of helping me out, all he could give me was a biased philosophical account of self-worth. How people were out to ruin other's chances of success, and also giving his personal testimony. I laughed to myself when I realized that was the common style of religious preaching in Kenya. He had really got me on that.

Out of necessity, we took a detour to town, instead of his place. His girlfriend wanted him to get her sandals from there. I had no other option, so we began our walk. My journey of a single step to town had already begun with the already stepped thousand miles from Colline Buffle. I was in for sore feet that day. I had to admit that getting sore feet was better than having peer pressure around me, like 'get drunk'. I wasn't ready to become an alcoholic just yet.

We reached Moustique stadium. From the outside, all we could see were walls with diverse murals. Right from the end of the forest were government buildings. We had passed the hospital, it was very big—*l'hopital en dessous de la colline*. The only place where

Swahili had prominence in public signs was in Tanzanie. It was rare to see them in mainland Kenya. It came in as a surprise to see the murals written in it. They had algorithms for reporting rape cases, and a public awareness campaign against gender-based violence. I saw that as a good initiative. The pictures depicted the suffering of a woman—*the girl child in peril.*

My first guess was that whoever had done that remarkable paintwork, must have been paid a fortune. Unfortunately, they never received a single dime. In Nuée's words, the artist did that as part of his job proposal. His dream to make murals of all the walls went down the drain. That was a big blow coming from the county government, which was ready to blow millions on lavish parties, cars, and sex. That guy's fate had been sealed by some selfish and inconsiderate demagogues.

The next day, I had great plans. I had finally gathered my confidence. Joanne was a great girl who had blown my mind away. Most of my peers had encouraged me to have sex before I left for home. Joanne had come to my mind. After narrating to Nuée my challenge, he was more than happy to offer a helping hand to a brother in need. It was from him that I got to know there were dotted condoms. He called them so, but I assumed he was referring to the studded ones. In his opinion, condoms were a wet blanket which spoiled all the fun. Using them was like eating candy with its plastic wrapping on. I knew where he was going, but I would never take such a risk.

The day before, we had moved all over but had no luck finding sandals. Nuée's girl had been super upset. If she were that close to meeting him, she would sure skin him alive. Luckily, he had put his phone on *mode avion*. His motive had been total radio silence. I had met him earlier that morning. I had lots of plans that day. From saying my final goodbyes to Ardente's family, and to keep a promise to take Jacqueline's girls to the Macérage, I had a lot on my plate. I, however, sat with Nuée for a while before leaving him. It was a good thing Ardente was around that day. I spent some time with him before heading to where Nuit and the others were.

I had handed them my dirty laundry that morning. I didn't want to go back home with a set of dirty clothes. Réveiller had been overly helpful. At the Macérage, were all kinds of people. I arrived when Jacqueline was doing final touches on her washing. She had already set aside several buckets of water, all for her. She said her body was her temple, and it needn't be dusty. I was amazed by her lexical puzzler. It seemed simple, but more complex the more one came to think of it.

I left them for a bit when I noticed Maman was not around. I had grown too fond of her. I felt my day as incomplete if I hadn't witnessed her shenanigans. I went around the huge water pan in search of her. There were women shamelessly taking baths, butt naked, in broad daylight. As a self-professed pervert, I shied away from taking a sneak peek at them. They seemed to care less. I was told that if I attempted to get close to them, then hell would break loose—*I was content with it staying intact.* Small boys were using makeshift rafts to sail around. Despite the water being relatively small, I wouldn't dare try their feat. Life was short, and

I wasn't ready to shorten it with sheer stupidity.

After what seemed like forever, I couldn't find Maman. When I got to where her mother was, there she was. She laughed at first, telling me how she hid in a bush next to where her mom was. She wanted to see me suffer a little, for the fun of it. I stood next to them while chatting about the recent headlines hitting the nation. Three girls were making the news. Two were identical twins, switched at birth, and they had found a piece to the missing puzzle. That shocking revelation had spawned controversy. I wasn't surprised of hearing that most of the major media houses, the court, and the Five-O had been involved. I paid less attention to news like that. The zeal with which Jacqueline had in discussing it was inspiring. One could think they were her daughters or close acquaintants.

I had been to the Macérage before, with Réveiller and Nuit. Public showers were not new to me. At that time I had acted all macho. The result was my arms hurting, after carrying forty pounds of water in each hand. I couldn't let myself suffer through the same fate again. It was a good thing Maman and I were tasked with porting the wet clothes in buckets. We left her mother prepping herself for a shower.

Time went by fast that day. I hadn't noticed, but the evening had come. We were busy watching a Nigerian film, with Nuit and her groupie, until the concept of time faded away into our fantasy. I was engrossed in the watching until Joanne came in. She wore black tights and a tiny dress. I looked at her in lust. Her well-combed afro-hair made her look great. We talked for a while before she mentioned she would be going to the flour mill at Virgule. I felt excited but I held my enthusiastic pressure deep inside. I watched her in infatuation as she talked to Réveiller. The latter came up to me with a proposal, she was inviting me to be her plus one in her journey to the flour mill—*it sounded a little poetic when I thought of it.*

I tried hard to come up with every possible pick up line I could, but all was futile. My small-talk skills were dwindling with every step of the way. It was a great thing that Réveiller was around, I wondered what would have happened if she were someplace else. I would have blown things out of proportion. I helped her carry a bucket of corn. Her over-dressing made me look a little out of her league. We made cuts through corn farms, and also passed through people's homes. It was not a big issue—*the folks around there were pretty much into socialism.*

I got jealous when one of the teens, from where I charged my devices, came over and held Joanne by the waist. He looked at me with a grin, and then dragged her into a nearby crowd of delinquents. Knowing that I was too old to stoop to his level, I quietly waited for Réveiller and headed home with her. It was until we had walked a few yards that Joanne joined us. She had a guilty-conscience look in her face. I acted as if nothing had happened, but deep down, I was losing my cool. I could notice cumulonimbus clouds gathering; all in anticipation to deliver—*it was not clear however, who was the dad.*

Before we knew it, the rain had started pouring in torrents. I assured the girls that all would be fine. My calmness prompted them to walk with me without haste. Albeit my strong heart, they quickly started taking to their heels. It was a leg-spare-me situation. With Joanne catching up to my pace, we managed to leave Réveiller a few meters behind. As we ran, I could feel my inner self urging me to tell Joanne something. I strongly ignored it and continued. After what seemed like an eternity of spirited running, the latter took a detour on one of their farms, and then, it was me and Réveiller against the world. I saw her silhouette disappear in the approaching darkness, a figure of a being growing darker and darker.

Réveiller and I were all wet. We sat comfortably in a couch designed for ten. It was so huge that we couldn't fit in it even with our legs stretched apart. The owner had been so generous to call us in. After Joanne had left us to the mercy of the storms, we were lucky that the old-timer had seen us while closing his gates. He was mad at us for not taking shelter soon enough. 'What are neighbors for?' He asked.

While taking shelter, I got into a one on one with Réveiller. From what I gathered, she was a kind and honest girl. Our host was a former police officer who hung his boots on the wall, like a picture. There was something strange about his house. A part of it had been recently extended, half the walls were plastered and the others not so. A glimmer of hope came when the rain suddenly stopped pouring intensely. Light showers hit the roof faintly, I knew it was time to leave. Despite our host acting nicely, I couldn't wait to leave his excuse of a home.

Réveiller and I had created a rapport so much that we began sharing our secrets. I told her of how I had more lives than a cat—*the many times my heart got broken was proof enough.* I walked her quietly home while waiting for the night to come. It was my last day there. I had to say my last goodbyes before it was too late. I partly regretted not having visited my uncle and aunt. They were the black sheep of the family, and getting to meet them would have been an honor. I tried to cherish every last step. It would be a long time coming before I would ever think of coming back.

I sat idly on a bench, it was eleven o'clock in the evening. My feet were all damp and muddy. I had stepped into a puddle accidentally. The pitch darkness had obstructed my view. Next to me was Joanne. She wore a baseball jacket and a short dress. One would have thought we were attending a soirée. Réveiller sat in front of us. Joanne and I whispered to each other, ignoring what the speaker was saying. Several girls sitting at our vicinity looked at us with hate, it looked as if we were interrupting their heavenly moment. We were in a church hall. Réveiller had invited me to attend a dance, hosted by one of the churches in her neighborhood. I hadn't attended one of those in years, it felt nice to at least be a teenager once again.

There were rowdy youths all over. Some of them carried with them weapons, from simple clubs to machetes. Knowing that I was walking with two girls, I had a hunch that things could get messy at any time. I wanted to be their protector, however, acting all tough in a foreign land wasn't that good—*might've hurt a bit*. Most of them sat in groups, discussing their prospects of dancing with the girls around.

After getting back home earlier, I went to Nuée's place and said my farewell. His mother and Ardente's were all sad. I tried to tell them I would be back before they even knew it, but they could hear none of it. On the other side, Jacqueline filled me up with countless tales, which I tried very much to ignore. That night was very somber. Béatrice took to listening to her tiny radio receiver. I looked at her in admiration, the mother I never had. From the way she handled her dear old Jacques, I knew all would have been great if I were her son.

That night earlier, the air had been filled with misty chills. I wore my sweater, but I could still feel the not so gentle embrace of the cold, *très froid*. I would have welcomed warmly the good old days; back when fireplaces were a thing. I tried hard to adapt to the harsh cold by rubbing my fingers against each other. It was all for nothing. Jacqueline didn't take it lightly when her daughter announced she would be going for a dance. Her voice of refusal echoed across the whole village. Réveiller, however, assured me that all would be well.

After tireless pleading and no approval, the latter made the final choice of rebellion. She and Joanne went over to the gates. I was left alone in the house begging Jacqueline to let me join them. After making a cute puppy face, my eyes were all googly and shiny, she finally let me out. I joined the others with a sense of pride. I wore sandals, which were a huge bummer, considering it was muddy. The three of us maneuvered the roads in the pitch darkness. My phone had a very dim torchlight, it was no use. As a clever excuse, I held Joanne by the waist and asked her to be my guide. She seemed fine with it.

Back at the church, there was less action. I suggested we leave earlier, but the duo wouldn't have it. They still had a glimmer of hope that somehow the dance would be on. An hour and a half later, the session was ended. We were told to leave for our homes, and that the dance would start the following day. I felt infuriated for the first time that night. It was my final day, and those guys hadn't the slightest clue how they had messed me up. As everyone dispersed, I saw the rowdy youths spread out quickly before their catches went out of reach. I prayed hard that they wouldn't get closer to Réveiller, « *Au nom du pére, et du fils, et du saint esprit ...*»

Joanne was the first to get mixed into a crowd of a dozen guys. Each of them had at least an assortment of unconventional weapons. Réveiller went over to a friend of hers, wielding a baseball bat, it seemed I was not enough protection for her. I took the insult heavily. She came over to where I was and held my hand, leading me to the road. It seemed obvious that she wouldn't introduce me as her uncle. In most cases, I would have better passed for as her brother. I bit my lip in silence when I saw one of the boys spank Joanne, and give her a light kiss on the cheek. I knew what I was getting into—*that girl was bad news.*

I recounted her tales of breaking curfew and sneaking out of her house, whenever there were dances. In as much as I thought it was teenage pressure, she had gone overboard. I had no kids, but my parental instincts had started kicking in. If she were my daughter, I would have sent her to boarding school, and given her a daily dose of shrink therapy. Réveiller's friend suggested we take a different route from what *la population générale* was... Before we knew it, Joanne had caught up with us. She gave an elaboration of the plight of women. I didn't see the correlation between that and what she had been doing—*her pain was self-*

100

inflicted.

True to the mystery guy's words, no one followed us. Our shortcut, which cut through farms and homesteads, was very ideal. He seemed very platonic with Réveiller. I didn't see any slight hand-holding. The way they interacted seemed all fine by me. Not wanting to look awkward prompted me to grab Joanne's waist again, and touch her whole body as we walked. It was a very pleasant experience. Over the years, I came to cherish the emotional connection I made with the girls I would meet. It was like sharing a piece of my soul with them.

Knowing that we would reach home in a matter of minutes, I came up with a master plan. I managed to convince Réveiller that it was okay for me to escort Joanne to her gate. I figured that would be the only alone time we were to have—*the last things I ever wanted were regrets*. I had everything planned out. The night sky was foggy. There was however bright moonlight, seeping its way through the atmospheric blanket. I walked the lady and then stood a few yards from her gate. I told her to stop and then held on to her waist again while looking her in the eye. She smiled at me and then moved closer to where I was. In a flash of a second, I had forgiven her past offenses against me. Our minds and bodies were in complete sync. I could hear our heartbeats and breathing, from a far distant, their pounding started getting louder.

If I were a passionate romantic, then I would have done great things for her. However, I bent in for a kiss. The air went all silent, apparently awaiting the greatest kiss ever. I closed my eyes as I felt her warm breath come straight to my nostrils. It was a heavenly moment. Before I knew it, she had pushed my cheeks aside, and then mumbled something about never kissing people on her first date—*maybe she planned on kissing zero frogs in hope of finding her prince charmant.* The feeling was not mutual, and it felt like the tempo had been set to zero.

I accepted her choice and then gave her a bear hug. We talked while listening to her not-so-interesting stories. As the cold continued beating us, we held on to each other closely. We would occasionally let go whenever Réveiller would come to where we were while announcing that it was getting late. Her constant reminders made our talks go off course. Like a house of cards, the little connection we were building was being shaken from its solid foundations.

In two hours, I got to know her in detail. I promised I would visit in August. She made a vow to kiss me for real on that day. I held on to that hope. Our final parting was standing while holding hands, and waiting for the wet blanket. It didn't take long before our separator came. At that time, the club was in her hands—*she meant business.* We walked silently to her home. I guessed everyone was dead asleep. However, her soft knock at the door was immediately responded to by Jacqueline. She looked at us half-approvingly and then let us in. Her words were, 'you'.

Fast forward a few months later at a time like that when I had come back, the girls were in school. Maman was the only one around. As we were taking our nap, we heard screams outside.

A Daunting Jaunt

An old lady was crying at the top of her lungs. We couldn't hear her exact words, but we could feel her pain. Her intonation did all the work. Jacqueline's sister in law was the first to meet us outside. We had convened for a small ensemble, discussing what was happening in the outside. She held on to her son, papa. He was crying his lungs out. It seemed his mother had destroyed his perfect baby dreams. From my telekinetic powers, I could hear his mind call her, *le contre-torpilleur.*

We headed to where the screams were coming from. The once faint sounds had now grown louder. I realized they were coming from near Joanne's home. I would have killed myself if it was her that was dead. I walked half afraid. It was through experience that I would shy away from attending events like that. At one time, I had come into a head-on collision with a gang. I didn't want to witness history repeating itself. It was a good thing the people around were all friendly. I dared not talk to the locals, lest they speak to me in an incomprehensible tongue. I was looking out around, and people were coming in from all directions.

I hadn't noticed, but Béatrice was a tall woman. From her old pictures, I could gather that her husband was of the same height as my dad, 5'10". However, her sons were super tall. It must have been her genes. Her Masai covering and hat made her silhouette echo across the darkly lit path. We all walked in a single file behind her, like ducklings after mother duck. We walked to a small home, where the screaming and ululations were at their highest. An old lady walked around in remorse and grief. He plight got us into grief. We took shade under banana trunks. Béatrice went over to where the other old hags were. They sat in a row of finely arranged bricks—*the construction plans were about to be halted.*

The home comprised of several mud houses, in blocks facing each other. The most notable one lay next to where we stood. On our left was an incomplete brick house. Everything was in place except for its doors, windows, and interior décor. Aside from the fact that the houses were mud-walled; they had excellent furnishings. From a completely solar-powered lighting system to finely crafted couches, I was impressed. For a second, I had forgotten people were in mourning.

I was told that we had to wait until the home's head came in—*you guessed right, it was a man.* It was said that he once married a lady, who he later divorced. He later remarried a middle-aged gal who had grown sons. It seemed for the very least that he was there for comfort. Considering he was living large in *Le port de Florence*, he had quite forgotten about his home. Then came a time when he found his gal cheating on him. As any less reasonable man would act, he opted to use a blunt knife and stab her in the head. What followed were countless court cases and fines. The gal's sons had sworn to bury him alive if they found him. He took to hiding in his home; where he waited for the occasional court summons, and with life became too hard for him.

If things couldn't get any better, his first wife called in. She was critically sick. Her wish was to get back to her husband once she had reached full recovery. Things went well for a while. She had gotten back to her feet and even visited her old flame. They rekindled their lost love and even mended their family relationships once again. It was one of the greatest things that ever happened to him, in light of his stabbing miseries.

However, a fortnight before, when the lady went back to her home and stayed for a while. She enjoyed a whole two weeks with her family, all in full health. However, tragedy struck, it was the last of everyone's expectations. Like a fiery wind out of nowhere, she took her last breath. The exact details of her passing were hidden from us, but I guessed it was probably in her makeup room—*it seemed that the only good thing coming out of her death was her looking pretty in the afterlife*. The people from there had heard the sad news and were all in tears. That was the reason why we heard the screams initially. I felt more pity for them which made me try hard but I couldn't drop any tear in my face. I chanted a silent mantra which lingered in my head; '*Watashi, gozen. Yori oki, yori. Jibuno, mondai.*'

From where we stood was a group of five men discussing. Most of them were busy staring at their phones. Their heights impressed me. Standing at about six foot one was the shortest guy of them all. While standing, his head was at the shoulder level of the tallest guy there. I cursed myself for never having those awesome genes. As I was thinking out loud, I heard everyone suddenly burst into laughter. One of them had told his friend, that he would beat him up until he farted. People around were looking for a way to let out a simple laugh, they provided that avenue. It was closure in its own.

The old lady's screams grew louder. I felt sympathy for her. She moved all over in song and tears. Her song was her inner turmoil finally let out loud. She wore a *tissu enveloppant*, which she folded to the middle of her legs. It felt heartwarming to see her fine legs, which looked nice without waxing—*I knew my thoughts were going overboard*. In her hand was a portable lamp, which was symbolic to the light the dead had on her. I focused on hearing her words:

mayo, elle est morte

mayo, elle était la lumière dans ma vie

A Daunting Jaunt

mayo, elle était la meilleure

Qu'elle repose avec ses pères

mayo, elles est morte

oh, mayo, ma fille

oh, mayo, ma fille, elle est morte.

Her song was a verse about her daughter's death, her light in her world, and a wish for her to rest with her fathers. After an hour of experiencing a free performance with countless encores, I got bored with the monotony. The lady too shared my sentiments, I saw her head to one of the houses. Surprisingly, I didn't see her leave afterward. We waited for forever, until we heard the blaring sounds of motorcycle horns. That was it, the owners had come.

They came in a swagger. The motor-bicycles were halted a hundred meters from the house; a rope was tied to each of their handles. One of the riders pushed while the other pulled. It was a spectacular view. My mouth was all agape when I saw them. A man and a woman were in front of them, screaming and wailing as if hell had landed on earth. In a nick of time, the old verse lady sprang from her hiding and joined them. It was *mayo* all over again. My desire for no more encores had finally been fulfilled. It was a good thing that after they had settled down, Béatrice signaled us to get going. I made a huge sigh of relief. It was good to be back to my bed, after all, I had something to do later the following day.

Fast rewind back to the present, I was woken up by my inconsiderate alarm clock. The D-day had finally come. I would be leaving my exclusive getaway. I had escaped to a temporary fantasy, and I was getting back to my reality. The harsh urban life: polluted streets, the reckless drivers, … I could fill-up the world's databases with my criticisms on it. Jacqueline had already set aside a jug of warm water for me. I laughed to myself when I realized it was meant for washing my face.

I had packed most of my stuff, the previous day, on Jacques's trunk. I knew beforehand that convenience would matter the most in the morning. Jacques had made a rigid excuse of not coming to pick me up. His reasons were that he was to visit the county offices on official business. I knew that was a flat lie. I ensured everything was all set before I left. It was a good thing I had carried two pairs of rubber shoes. In light of the philanthropic spirit, I handed over one to Nuit. The look of gratitude in her face was payment enough. She was very happy.

As I was tying my last lace, Béatrice came over to where I was. I anticipated a final call for farewell, but to my surprise, she asked whether I had left the sandals they had loaned me. I looked at her with a look that said 'hey-is-this-a-joke?', before I pointed to where they were. Her question was very ill-placed. My quick temper prompted me to take my bag and leave at once. My ego had been bruised, and I was not yet ready to nurse any wounds just yet.

I got to Jacques's place at exactly seven-thirty. The lawn was damp with dew. I could almost feel the moistness take a hold of my feet. I had worn rubber shoes for the whole course of my journey. I knocked on his door with a mixture of eagerness and tension. I was glad that the most awaited day had finally come. I would go home and recount all the wonderful times I had over there. After waiting impatiently at the door; Jacques's wife opened it, she took a close look at me. Out of courtesy, I said, 'hi' to her. She half gazed at me and then closed the door. I guessed it was so because I had soiled her lobby. It seemed I had gathered lots of moss during my long trek.

After leaving Béatrice's place, I walked away in fury. On my way, I met with an old man, who claimed he was my father's peer. He described him as being a tall guy—*who had been very naughty*. His tales revolved around him smacking my dad and them being mortal enemies. I made a promise I would deliver his greetings but solemnly swore not to live up to his expectations. I walked the road with him, half-wishing that the earth would give rise to T-Rex's, which would devour him to the last marrow.

I watched the door slam after the lady. She had made a statement. I waited patiently while scrolling through my phone. It was the least I could do in the midst of all that was unfolding. To my relief, Jacques opened the door and let me in. My hate for his wife started germinating from the ground up—*a little sunlight, and water would do a neat trick*. The house was no different from before. The only noticeable thing was the change of seat covers. I sat relaxed on one of the couches. Étienne was busy packing stuff in the car. I liked the fact that he took several bottles of water from the fridge. The rest were snacks, dried fish, and yew! I liked the first bits, but leftovers from their last meal, that was so not good.

The table was packed with chapati, baguettes, croissants, and milk. It was fun to finally have a *thé avec du lait* experience. Knowing that his wife had acted less of herself, I only took a cup of hot milk and then left. It was enough that my respect was tarnished, I wasn't ready to let my dignity … I decided that people thinking they could see you like trash, and then offering you meals, wasn't all that exciting. I looked at Étienne with renewed interest. He was not the kind of person you would call a *camarade—his loyalty lay elsewhere.*

The only thing that made me keep my cool was Heureux. In spite of her mother acting so evil, a smile from the kid made my heart warm. At first, she gave me her teddy bear, and then one of her Barbie dolls. She kept running around while holding my arm. I felt a spark of joy for once. I said to myself that sometimes, even evil things could create innocence, or maybe ignorance was a bliss.

Before I knew it, we were past Moustiquen lands. I was in a deep sleep. True to my words, Jacques didn't leave for official business that morning. His excuse was just another one of his lies, which I had learned to keep up with. I held on to my nape while in deep thought. It was a long time since I placed too much attention on deciphering human nature. We did have the company of someone quite familiar that day. Professeur had joined us for a trip to Naïrobi. Étienne and I took the back seats. I liked those spots the most—*I could sleep at will.*

For a moment, I saw Félicité before me. She wore a loose cotton dress. I felt drawn to her the longer I kept gazing. Her image began to blur the more I thought of it as surreal. I held on to my thoughts and then continued with my daydreaming. However, the more I tried to dismiss her, the more she appeared vividly. I finally gave in to her. She had an unusual face. It was bright yellow and had acne written all over it. Her now shorter hair looked more appealing than ever. I took the time to study her features. I didn't care that it was a fantasy, she looked real to me.

My thoughts later came in flashes. After hooking up with Cécile, our fallout began. I still nursed wounds from my previous rejection. The former had already chained herself into a life commitment—s*ocial media was filled with her lovemaking captions.* I met the latter on several occasions, but I couldn't have any regrets. The radiance in her face spoke of confidence. At one time, I passed her by. Having had no recent intimacy, I felt a little offended when I saw a guy caressing her cute face. I tried hard not to play the jealousy card.

However, I was all over her several days later. Albeit my focus; my love for her was like a one-way street, a single alley that led to zero interest in me. The guy in question had barely finished his O'Levels, and there he was—*my competition.* My constant bother led her to dismiss my undying love in public. Her exact words were, 'Hey, Reveur, "Get out of my face!"' The scene had been set in an evening stage. Flowers were glowing in the orange sunset. A cool breeze swept in the air. Like a stalker, I followed her quietly while she was having her moments, with my nemesis. After what seemed like an eternity, the guy left. It was us against the world. My folly had prompted me to showcase my dancing moves in front of her. Little did I know she hated publicity stunts. That was our end. As I left, the flowers' glow began to dim, and everything finally came to a halt.

My journey down memory lane wasn't all that fulfilling. I woke up to Étienne's tap on my shoulder. He whispered to my ear that there were police all over. My first response was, "I ain't know nothin'" Traffic police came over to where we were. Jacques was calm and confident. After the usual request for license and registration, he promptly gave them out. I watched as the officer shed a tear internally. He was hoping for a bribe—*his only challenge was finding us a mistake and not being smart enough to craft one.* We drove off speedily on the highway, maintaining below eighty kilometers per hour. It was the Easter season, and so, many roadblocks were put up. It seemed there was a correlation between recklessness and holiday-making.

We made a stop at Naroque town. Jacques made a stop directly at a *boucherie*, it was like a roadside fast food joint. The only difference being that it served long-distance travelers. I was starving, and I could swear, eating a bison wouldn't be any problem. I followed the pack, with Jacques leading it. We were like tourists on the move. Our distinct styles and accents sold us out. The place was like a huge parking lot for highway cars, and a food joint too. From the entrance, one could see several buses, and automobiles all lined up. After the cars, there were barbecue stands all over. I was particularly interested in sampling the different meats on display. My heart was dying to try out mutton.

The other day, there was news making headlines, of a guy who supposedly sold human meat. I wasn't a great fan of watching the bulletins; but the vivid description I got from a lady in the village, got me fully on board with the story. It was said that the guy in question, chopped off people's limbs, scrapped their skin off, and then sold the juicy flesh. Since it was rumored that some of the Ougandais tribes were cannibals, it would be no surprise seeing them flooding the guy's place—*all in effort to get his business card.* In as much as I liked theorizing on conspiracies, my watering mouth said otherwise.

We walked to 'our' car with haste. Jacques had calculated a major storm about to hit us. If we were to make it in time, then getting past the nine kilometer stretch of escarpments, would be a great idea. The last thing he would ever want was for us getting marooned in the middle of the road—*we would be at the mercy of bandit hyenas if they did exist.* I had carried with me, leftovers. Back at the *boucherie* we had ordered two pounds of chicken, a mountain of *xima*, and salad. Everyone ate to their fill and left. I, on the other hand, decided it was not so great to fatten the already fat cats—*they were all over us as we ate.*

The journey went on all smoothly, without any police in our way, all until we were fifty miles from Naïrobi. A police officer signaled us to stop. We expected some cooked up charges in store for us, and I could see the chills in everyone's faces. Luckily for us he was hitching for a ride. He was full of tales from when he started the service to some time which I would never bother to recall. It took him only five minutes, uninterrupted, to give us his full oral-biography. As a side note, he hinted to us that it was cold, and he was looking for a lady to keep him warm. We all laughed at his comment before he left. His departure left us in total silence until we finally saw the cliché of our city and its famous bottle like building, *Le Centre de conférences International du Kenyatta.*

From there, Professeur complained of how the government had invested greatly in infrastructure in cities near the *metropolie*, and not in places like Moustique. I looked forward to getting back. Dusk was kicking in, and we were not very far from reality. I watched in silence, as my one-time façade was fading away. If I were to turn back time, then it would have been a week earlier. The others would have however differed with my view. It seemed like my golden experience was only subjective. Étienne looked at the faraway skyscrapers in anticipation. His thoughts were revolving on how he would get back to his family. Jacques was confident that his cozy house was waiting for him. I, on the other hand, was anxious about where I would lay my head next.

The clouds suddenly darkened. We had experienced light showers on our way a few hours earlier. It seemed likely that we were in for a rainy homecoming. The sky suddenly lost its orange sunset radiance. All was left was darkness hovering above us. A chilly breeze swept through the tiny car windows, that was it. The Naïrobien dry spell was finally over.

La fin

Glossary

- *Organisation des Nations Uniés :* the United Nations.

- STI: sexually transmitted infection.

- «Je vais bien merci.» I am fine thank you

- «Je ne comprends le francais pas, vous parlez lentement.» I don't understand French, please speak slowly.

- «Bonne soirée mademoiselle,» Have a good evening, lady.

- Mph : Miles per hour

- *La Vie Demi du Naïrobi :* The Nairobi Half Life.

- coiffeur's : hairdresser's

- *Jeune Personne:* A younger/subordinate person.

- Les terres de Naïrobi est: Nairobi East Lands

- Le jeu des trônes: the game of thrones

- *Une douzaine de personnes:* A dozen people

- *Les Derniers en Appellant:* The last ones in calling.

- *le salle de bain:* Washroom

- *Au revoir:* Good bye

- *À demain:* see you tomorrow

- *le salle de sport:* Sports room/place.

- *je n'ai pas compris:* I didn't understand.

- *Vallée de Rift:* the Rift Valley

- *Tranquilité:* calmness.

- *Pattisseries: pastries*

- *Thé sans lait:* tea without milk

- *Thé avec du lait:* tea with milk

- *Sur contrôle:* in control

- *Viande contre la viande:* sex without protection.

- *Félicitations:* congratulations.

- *Douche:* shower

- *Fantôme de Ne Pas:* Phantom of Ne Pas.

- *vingt quatre sur vingt quatre:* 24/7

- *à l'instant :* At the moment

- *le repas :* the meal

- *spectaculaire :* spectacular

- *excellent eclairage nocturne :* excellent eye care night lighting.

- *Omelette espagnol :* Spanish omelette

- *Les américains :* Americans

- *outils :* tools

- *magnifique :* magnificent

- *«Je m'appèle Heureux»* : I am called Heureux.

- *«Non, tu es Heureux pas. Je suis Heureux, je suis Heureux, … »* : "No, you're not Heureux, I am Heureux …"

- *«Salut, je voudrais charger mon ordinateur, m'aider s'il te plaît.»* : "Hi, I would like to charge my computer, help me please."

- *«Aller au salon … » :* "Go to the sitting room."

- *«Merci … »* : "Thank you …"

- *la vie facile* : the easy life.

- *Fixez vos ceintures de sécurité* : Fasten your safety belts.

- *«Ne repose pas sur le jardin»* : Don't rest on the garden

- *«Je suis entrain de regarder»* : I am watching

- *Olamiri et le Crocodile* : Olamiri and the Crocodile

- *tissu enveloppant* : Wrap free fabric

- *Le règlement rural kenyan* : the Kenyan reserve (rural settlements)

- *hors du combat* : out of the fight.

- *Le Coin Mortel* : the deadly corner.

- *Je n'ai pas de souffrance* : I don't have any problems.

- *l'hopital en dessous de la colline* : the hospital below the hill

- *mode avion* : airplane mode

A Daunting Jaunt

- *très froid* : very cold

- « *Au nom du pére, et du fils, et du saint esprit*
  ...» : In the name of the father, and of the
  son, and of the holy spirit, …

- *la population générale* : the general
  population

- *prince charmant* : prince charming

- *le contre-torpilleur* : the destroyer

- '*Watashi, gozen. Yori oki, yori. Jibuno,
  mondai.*' : 'I am bigger than my problems'

-
  mayo, elle est morte

  mayo, elle était la lumière dans ma vie

  mayo, elle était la meilleure

  Qu'elle repose avec ses pères

  mayo, elles est morte

  oh, mayo, ma fille

  oh, mayo, ma fille, elle est morte.

- *transcription:*

Mayo, she is dead

Mayo, she was the light in my life

Mayo, she was the best

May she rest with her fathers

Mayo, she is dead

Oh, Mayo, my daughter

Oh, mayo, my daughter, she is dead

- *boucherie :* meat selling shop

- *Le Centre de conférences International du Kenyatta :* The Kenyatta International Conference Center

- *metropolie :* metropolis

- *La fin :* the end